Frances Gorham

2-14

S0-ADG-678

Goshen College
Library

TWO THIEVES

BOOKS BY MANUEL KOMROFF

———

CORONET

JUGGLER'S KISS

THE GRACE OF LAMBS

MANUEL KOMROFF

TWO
THIEVES

PUBLISHED IN NEW YORK BY
COWARD - Mc CANN, Inc.
IN THE YEAR 1931

Goshen College
Library

COPYRIGHT, 1931, BY
MANUEL KOMROFF

All Rights Reserved

MANUFACTURED IN THE U. S. A.

PS
3521
05.3
T9

13602

PZ
3
357
To

TO

BELLE AND BEN MICHAILOVSKY

TWO THIEVES

I

PONTIUS PILATE ruled Judea with an iron hand.
Roman justice for all. Greek, Arab and Jew met in
his court, and Roman soldiers, housed in the stone
barracks beneath the long halls of the Holy Temple, were ready at any moment to see that his word
was law.

The Greek merchants complained of the heavy
taxes but their protests were brushed aside. The
cunning Arabs fled to the desert and here, in the
ancient sands of their birth, even here they were
harried and driven before Roman lance and shield.
And the high Jewish priests in the Holy Temple
were stripped of their power. Their sacred vest-

9

ments, the holy jewelled breast-plate and their most cherished vessels of devotion were taken from them and locked up in a tower of the palace. Pilate himself held the key and opened the door only on holy days to lend out the various objects and robes needed for the special service, but at the end of the day he made certain that everything was returned and the iron-bound door of the strong room securely locked.

Only in one thing did he fail. The golden eagles of his Emperor and the proud military banners that he brought from Rome and set up on the tall towers of his palace, these he was forced to remove. Jewish tradition would allow no images to come into the Holy City. Crowds gathered on the first day of their appearance. The protests turned to threats and soon the people grew into a surging mob, stronger than the whole legion of soldiers at Pilate's command. The eagles and the banners came down. In all things he could rule, except against this holiest tradition. Against what the Jews called imagery he was powerless.

At last peace from outer enemies had been secured but at the end of the fourth year of his rule, soon after he began the building of a great stone waterway which should bring fresh water from several of the great desert cisterns into the very heart of Jerusalem, in the early spring of this year, his troubles began.

It started with a single incident. Pilate received a report from the chief builders of this waterway and he was displeased. "In Rome it would have been finished long before!" he cried. He bit his lips and was silent, for his anger endured but a moment. He knew that Judea was not to be compared to Rome, and he knew that an aqueduct through a desert was a task greater than one between two of the Seven Hills. He knew also that the climate was hot and that water and provisions had to be dragged long distances over hills of sand to keep the army of ten thousand slaves at work. Moreover, a thousand slaves died every year and these had to be replaced. Already half of the Temple treasure, against the cries and protestations of the priests and the populace, had been spent on this noble project.

Finally he decided to send one of his trusted captains, a veteran of many wars, a Roman of stern character, named Marcus Sulla, whose grand-uncle was a famous general, to assist the commander and put strict discipline into the gangs of slaves.

Sulla put aside his heavy sword, wrapped a long chariot whip about his girdle and set off with great determination. He was gone only one week and when he returned he was a broken man and so changed in appearance that Pontius Pilate himself barely recognized him. When he went, he drove out of Jerusalem in a bronze chariot drawn by two fiery Arabian horses. His polished leather breast-plate studded with brass nails glistened in the sun. But he returned on foot, sore, limping, with face bruised, mouth bleeding, body black and blue, dazed, inarticulate and hardly able to put one foot before the other.

It had all happened in a very simple way. When Sulla arrived in this fine chariot at the place where the main work was being done, which was nothing more than a camp in the desert about ten leagues south of Jerusalem, he at once presented himself to the commander-in-chief. This official was not overpleased with Sulla's arrival but pretended that he was glad of any military aid.

The next morning Sulla set to work. He went
from one gang to another and installed a new sys-
tem of punishments, severe and drastic, for all
kinds of petty offenses. The lazy were to be beaten
into activity. The sick were to be cured with the
medicine of the rod. And to show that he was
in earnest Sulla made the whole camp eat their
midday meal while standing, and those who at first
dared disobey and from weariness sat upon the
ground, they were brought forward and kicked
and beaten, so that those who would not stand now
were senseless and unable to rise from the ground.

The multitude growled like beasts in a trap,
but they had been beaten before and driven before
and burdened with work and now, if their very
weariness was given no rest, what did one more
thing really matter? Their spirit was crushed to
a pulp. Their arms hung limp and the chains
attached to the strong cuffs about their wrists
dropped almost to the ground. The noonday sand
was hot and they shifted from one bare foot to
the other.

On the third day Sulla, pleased with himself,
drove out in his chariot to visit one of the stone

quarries. Here his downfall began. A young Jewish slave, with black hair and sparkling eyes, was carrying a great boulder on his powerful shoulders. The muscles of his arms and back stood up in small hard lumps, and he passed boldly in front of Sulla, just as the Roman was shouting to a group of slaves and threatening them with his whip; and as he passed he laughed. He laughed out loud.

"Here, you!" cried the Roman. "Put that down!"

The young slave, he was barely twenty, turned around.

"Put that down and hear what I command!"

The slave came forward and dropped the great rock at Sulla's feet. So close was the drop that the officer jumped back in fright. Then he struck out with his whip but the slave snatched it out of his hand and it fell between them.

There was a moment when all was still. Then suddenly from behind the quarry rocks appeared an Arab merchant driving three heavily laden asses before him. "Go on there! Get along!" he cried to the beasts driving them ahead over the rocky bit of ground. But before they had made much

14

headway or could come into view, Sulla snatched the whip from the ground and lashed into the slave.

The first stroke landed squarely on his shoulders but the slave only laughed. The second cut into his face and lashed around his neck. Now the slave bent low and came a step forward. As the third stroke came full upon his back he suddenly threw out the chain that hung from his wrists. He cast it low and, snaring the captain's raised foot, upset his balance. Sulla fell on his back.

The Arab merchant forced his beasts ahead into the middle of this commotion. He poked their ribs with a little stick and cried: "Get on! Get along!"

At the same time the weary slaves who had stood in silence now took courage and broke into a joyous cry. They armed themselves with small stones.

Sulla recovered his feet and reached for a spear from the hand of the nearest soldier. The soldiers had begun driving back the slaves and threatening them with shield and lance. But before Sulla could reach for the weapon the young slave came forward and lifted the captain high in the air and held him in his powerful arms. The Roman shouted,

15

he called, he waved his arms, he kicked his legs
but the young slave held him tight. He cursed,
he tried to reach for his dagger but the crushing
arms of the slave pinned him close and he could
not wedge his hand between.

Soldiers rushed forward and saved the captain
from being hurled against the rocks. They tore
the two men apart and held the slave while Sulla,
red with fury, shook himself to relieve the sudden
pressure that had come upon his bones. Again he
reached for the whip; this time he held it by the
soft end and swung the handle forward. The soldiers threatened the slaves who, weak in spirit,
dropped the stones in their hands. But the Arab
had sent his loaded asses directly into the middle of
this scene.

"Away! Out of here!" Sulla cried and struck
the beast nearest him across the head. "Away!"

"Is this the road for Jerusalem?" The Arab
addressed the captain.

"Yes. Get on!"

"I am a stranger . . . a poor stranger. I want
to go to Jerusalem. You would not send me on
a wrong road?"

16

The crafty Arab put on an air of simplicity. But his eyes twinkled as he glanced at the young powerful slave held by the soldiers.

"I would send you to the devil himself if you do not get out of here at once. Out of my way!"

His whip flew out and he swung it over his head. The loaded asses took fright and turned away. The Arab himself followed and shouted out so all could hear; "We must have come at a bad moment." He drove his asses slowly out of the pit.

At the top of the rocks he turned and watched a celebrated Roman punishment. He saw everything. He saw them lead the slave away to the main camp where the commander had his tents and there the slave was chained to a tall stake. His hands were fastened high above his head and for lack of blood they became white as parchment. His legs could hardly stand yet they must or his arms held high and taut would be wrenched from their sockets.

At night while the Roman officers were drinking wine and singing bawdy songs the commander was called from his tent by one of the orderlies.

17

The Arab and his three laden asses stood before him. The moon was full over them.

"I am on my way to Jerusalem and I have need of a strong slave. The markets are at some distance and I thought that if you liked to aid a worthy traveller, you would find me ready to pay, and pay you well."

"What do you call well?"

"I can pay in silver."

The commander looked about to see that nobody was within hearing distance. "If your silver is soft and good there is nothing here that I would not give you."

The two men walked out of the shadow of the tent. The commander was silent but the look on his face showed plainly that there was nothing he would not sell. The face of the Arab was not quite so open. There was a twinkle in his eye that told of a crafty scheme and his smile was but the veil over something evil. His age was about fifty-five years but his brown leathery skin, parched by desert suns and his deeply lined face, weathered by wind and cut by the blowing sand, made him look

18

the timeless master of the rude and dark places of Judea. While the glance of his eye was youthful, everything else about him seemed old and hard as the rocks of his arid desert.

"How much will you pay?"

"Forty pieces of silver for a young fellow, strong and without blemish or illness, a body without sores and without a fault."

"Such a one is worth sixty but if you will take him now at night and if none of my officers see it, you can have him for fifty."

They walked into the enclosure where some of the slaves were encamped for the night.

"I want the fellow that was brought in from the quarries today."

"The young Jew. I promised him to Sulla. He wants to take him back to Jerusalem and give him a treatment in a pit."

"I will buy him."

"Take another one."

"No, I must have him."

"How can I account to Sulla?"

"Tell him he died and his body is gone."

"Give me seventy-five pieces of silver."

He counted them out one by one and they took down the slave.

"If you paid in gold, I would sell you even Sulla himself."

"We may yet return for him."

The commander laughed at this piece of banter, and went back into the tent.

The Arab unfastened the iron cuffs and cast off the chains. Then he helped the limp slave mount one of the asses and they drove out of the camp into the cool desert night on the road to Jerusalem.

II

LATE the following morning, refreshed by sleep and food, the Arab and the young slave rested in the shade of some tall palms. The three lazy asses, stripped of their packs, grazed not far off in a thorny patch of fen.

"Master," said the slave. "What must I do?"

"You will drive the asses. You will water them and give them feed. And at night you will set up the poles of the tent and make the fire."

"And we will go to Jerusalem?"

"Ah, there and other places. Many places."

"And you are a merchant and I will guard the packs?"

21

"Yes, you will, but the merchandise is not for ordinary traffic. We will buy and we will sell, but we seek not a profit of currency. The coin of our barter is neither silver nor gold. But in time you will know everything."

"And now we go to Jerusalem?"

"Possibly. My directions are not fixed. Are you anxious to be there?"

"No."

"And where do you come from?"

"It is there I once lived. But now I have nobody, nobody. My uncle sold me when I was thirteen. He was a merchant and he brought me up in his house, but he took to himself a second wife and I displeased her."

"And for that he sold you?"

"Yes, for that and the money. He is a miser and he counts his coins over every night."

"Perhaps we will visit him in Jerusalem."

"It is now seven years since I saw him and he may be dead."

"If he is dead then he deserves to be dead and if he is alive he ought to be dead." The Arab smiled at his own witticism.

"You are a good man," said the slave.

"No. You will not say I am good when you know me better. What is your name?"

"Rongus."

"And you are a Jew?"

"Yes."

"You read Hebrew?"

"Hebrew and Greek too. I had a Greek teacher. My parents loved me dearly. But they are both dead."

"And tell me, Rongus, one thing more. Did you have many masters?"

"No. Only the Romans."

"And you were seven years in the quarries?"

"No, only two. The rest of the time I was far in the desert with soldiers making war. We laid siege to many cities and I was the stroke-pull on a battering-ram. No, not at first. When I first came I was only a boy of thirteen and they set me on the ropes and water carrying."

"What ropes?"

"The log ropes on the battering-ram. They are so close together that when they are suddenly let loose, so that the log may pound against the wall,

they often cross and kink; but I would stand by
and run in and separate the strands. You had to
be quick, for the swinging log does not rest and
if you yourself got caught in this net of ropes,
your life would not be worth anything. In fact we
once caught one of our officers in the ropes and
the more he cried 'stop!' the harder we pulled; it
took half-an-hour before he was all dead. Perhaps
I should not tell you this?"

"Why not?"

"Because you may think I am an ordinary crim-
inal and now that you have brought me away and
saved me from a terrible punishment. . . . No, I
am not that. I will always be grateful to you."

"If you killed with your own hands a hundred
Romans it would please me better."

"I will serve you faithfully all my life."

"Not for long, Rongus. If things go well with
us you shall soon have your freedom."

They loaded the asses and drove on slowly. The
road lay between short limestone hills covered with
a low, thorny brush. They passed merchants driving their mangy camels and cursing because the
black pebbly gravel of the road offered poor foot-

ing for their over-laden and weary beasts. They
passed some rocky caves where white-skinned
lepers, forbidden under pain of death to enter any
village or mingle with any people, had taken
refuge. The Arab threw them a small bag of meal
and they raised their white arms out of their rags
and called down the blessings of heaven upon him.

They also journeyed through a sandy valley
where hermits lived in mud huts roofed with gray
olive branches. And one of these stood in his open
doorway and cried out his prophecies.

"All for a penny and a penny for all. And the
world will go as the penny goes. And silver and
gold will be the gods. Love and pity are for birds
and fishes; man is born in strife and in meek-
ness he must perish. All for a penny and a penny
for all."

The Arab tossed a coin and it fell at the feet of
the hermit.

Soon they arrived at the beautiful city of
Herodium, built in the manner of the Greeks by
Herod, the father of the present king of Judea.

From the gates of the city the main avenues

were flanked with columns and the streets were
graded and paved with stone. Colorful mosaics
decorated the public squares and there was an arena
for sports and games. The city contained a theater
built close to a small grove of tall date trees. Here
one could walk through a long flight of shallow
marble steps, to the public baths built by Greek
architects, but containing the Roman vapor halls
and cold water pools.

Beside the city was a sharp mound shaped like
a woman's breast. "Here," said the Arab, "is where
Herod is buried. On the very top concealed in a
grove of trees stands the granite tomb and in this
very tomb. . . . There, I might today be lying
dead beside him."

"Dead!"

"Yes. As close as a bit hangs to a horse's mouth
so close was my life to death and my corpse in the
tomb."

The slave did not question further. They journeyed through the wall of the city and put up at
one of the inns.

Rongus unloaded the packs and tied the animals
in the yard as far away from the camels as pos-

sible for he knew that there would be no peace between them.

.   .   .   .

In the meantime the Roman captain Sulla grew weary of shouting his measures of discipline to the plodding slaves building the waterway. His arm tired of cracking the whip and he quarrelled with the works-commander as well as with the other officers. He lost all his money playing dice with a rowdy crew in the barracks and he could find nobody willing to polish his leather corslet and his plumed brass helmet. Besides, it was hot and dusty and he longed for the comforts of Jerusalem. Therefore he concluded that he had accomplished his purpose and set out on his return journey.

He, too, took the road for Jerusalem and he arrived at Herodium a day after the Arab with his laden asses and his young slave, Rongus.

They would probably never have met again had it not been for a peculiar incident that occurred. As Rongus was coming out of the yard he noticed a young lad standing before the inn in the roadway. The lad stood quite still and soon Rongus

27

saw that he was carrying a thin iron rod to which
were fixed several iron rings. This was a blind-
beggar's staff; the rings would clank as he walked
and people hearing this sound would make room
and allow him to pass. The lad was blind and was
evidently waiting for someone to lead him across.

At that moment Sulla's beautiful bronze chariot
drawn by the two Arabian horses came pounding
down the paved avenue. Rongus threw up his arms
to signal to the driver; he was too far from the
blind youth to snatch him out of danger. Then
in a flash he made a rush for the horses and seizing
the head and reins of the outermost steed, with all
his might he turned the beast in the harness. This
sudden twist pulled both horses to the side of the
road and they rushed by the blind youth.

Sulla pulled on the reins with all his might.
Rongus hung on to the horse's head for if he had
let go he would have been trampled under the
hoofs. At last it all came to a stop and Sulla rushed
down from the chariot with whip in hand.

Suddenly he was face to face with the slave—
the very same who had thrown him only recently

28

and laughed in his face before the workers of the quarry—he recognized him and stood still in amazement.

At the same time a sad-eyed girl of about sixteen or seventeen, poorly clad, ran forward and threw herself on Rongus' neck and cried; "You saved him, you saved him! You saved my poor brother and I have nothing—nothing and am unable to reward you." Her face was fair and her large eyes reflected warm sympathy.

"Stand back!" cried Sulla. "Stand back!"

"It's not his fault. He saved my brother. Whip me instead," and she threw herself at the feet of the Roman officer.

"Stand back!"

But just then the Arab ran from the door of the inn; he ran to Sulla and cried; "The Lord has brought you in time. Blessed be the Lord. Before you say another word let me tell you that I have bought this slave only this week from a Roman and . . ."

"He had no right to sell him."

"I paid him in silver and I bought him as he stood and without a fault. But he is a thief and

29

I demand that you take him with you to the Roman court in Jerusalem."

"It cannot be true. It cannot be true," came from the girl.

"It is true. And as I bought him from a Roman so he must be tried before a Roman and not by a scribbling city clerk."

"And you, who accuse, will you come with us and make the charges?"

"I will."

"And you will appear before the judges?"

"Yes. He is a thief and he must be punished."

"Then by Jupiter, we will go. Together we will take him to justice."

"Master!" called Rongus. "Master! What have I done?"

"Silence!" cried the Arab. "Not a word from you!"

And so they left the girl sobbing in the street before the inn, and her blind brother stood there also.

Rongus stepped into the chariot. The Arab and the Roman, with his dagger drawn, stood behind him. In this manner they rode through the beautiful city of Herodium and out into the desert on the way to Jerusalem. But by winks and certain glances the shrewd Arab gave Rongus to understand that it was all a game. And the game was played in the following manner.

When they had travelled about a league, Rongus driving the horses and the Roman at his back with the dagger, the Arab said to the Roman; "I do not like his style of driving. He will upset us. Better take the reins yourself and I will hold him between us with your dagger."

The Roman surrendered his dagger and took charge of the horses. They went on in this way for another half league and when they saw that they were approaching a small village the Arab said; "Really, now I do not know which of you should be tried. At first I thought the slave was the thief, but now I think the commander was a cheat and perhaps we should go back to the water-works and return the slave and get back our money."

"The judges in Jerusalem will hear you. They will decide," said the Roman.

31

"And then perhaps it is you yourself who should be tried before them."

Now Sulla was growing a bit uncomfortable. He whipped up the horses. Rongus stood in silence and was puzzled, for he had no idea what was going on in the Arab's mind.

"Yes, I really think," continued the Arab, "that it is you who have taken the money and you have cheated me."

"The judges will decide. They will give you a chance to explain everything."

"Yes, it must have been you, for I saw you beat this same slave in the quarry and the commander surely sold him because you ordered him to do so."

"No, no! You are inventing stories that will be hard to prove, and the judges are severe on those who . . ."

"What judges?" cried the Arab.

"Our judges."

"Romans! And what chance have I in a Roman court and what chance has a Jew?"

"It is justice for all."

The chariot drove on madly.

"No, we will have our justice now. Here and now!"

And, with a sudden movement, the Arab snatched the brass helmet from the Roman and placed it on the head of his slave.

Now Sulla realized that he had fallen into a trap. The dagger was at his back. He already knew that in strength he was no equal to the slave. But now he also realized that in a battle of wits he was as a child compared to the Arab.

"Drive on!" commanded the Arab and he tore the purple toga from the shoulder of the Roman. Then the leather corslet was unstrapped and these he helped fasten on to Rongus.

Before arriving at the next village they stopped and cutting two straps from the leather reins, they tied Sulla hand and foot. Then they continued their journey and came into the village with loud cries of lamentation.

"Oh, my son! My son! What shall we do! Oh my son!" cried the Arab.

In a moment a crowd gathered.

"Oh, my son! My son! He is mad and his reason has flown. Oh, my son!"

In this way, they went on slowly through the streets until they came to the village barber. Into his yard they dragged the unwilling Sulla. A crowd followed them.

"These men are rogues. They are rogues and I am captain of . . ."

"My son. He is mad. Oh help us, help us."

"We must bleed him at once," said the barber.

"Bleed him—do anything only save my boy. He is jealous of his brother who is a soldier as you may see. All his life he has been jealous and all his life he wanted to become a soldier. But he was born with a weakness and he cannot tell the truth. He was the eldest and I kept him at home. My son! Oh, my son!"

"Don't touch me, you beasts. I am captain of the Tower guards and you will pay with your lives. They are rogues!"

"You see how he carries on. And the whole trouble began with the decay of his upper teeth. The rot from the roots entered the brain. And the physicians have advised drawing them out, only the upper row, but there is nobody where we live who can do such a service."

34

Then the barber spoke up proudly; "I have taken out more teeth with my pincers in this little town than any barber in the whole of Jerusalem." Saying this, he lifted Sulla's lip and counted eight teeth in the upper row.

"The Lord has brought me to the right place. You will save my son and I will pay you well. Here is a piece of silver for each of the eight teeth. Let us set to work at once. My son! Oh, my son! We will save you yet and reason will be restored."

"You will all pay," roared the maddened Sulla. "By Hercules, you will pay with your lives!"

But his hands and feet were held tight by the straps and the barber's assistants, spurred into activity by this great excitement, had already begun bleeding their patient. They sat upon him to hold him down.

This evil deed was accomplished in short time.

"He is exhausted, my poor son," said the Arab. "He needs rest. We will leave him with you for the night. We dare not move him now. Take good care of him and you will be well paid; here is gold coin and spare nothing. If he needs more bleeding then do not hesitate to do so. I place him in your hands with full confidence. And tomorrow we return. Oh, my son! My poor son. Pray to God that his reason may return."

With these words the Arab and his astonished slave stepped into the beautiful chariot and drove back to the proud city of Herodium.

III

THE Arab explained at the inn that the poor
Roman soldier was suddenly taken ill with con-
vulsive pains and that they left him in care of a
physician. They had returned in the bronze chariot.
And the Arabian horses were stabled in the yard.

As for Rongus, he went through the streets of
the city looking for the beggar girl, the one who
had thrown herself on his neck in gratitude. He
wanted her to know that he was not a thief and he
wanted to tell her what happened between the
Roman and himself in the quarry. He saw the
vision of her face before him, smooth and oval
with her large brown eyes as they filled with tears

and she cried; "It cannot be true. It cannot be true."

He searched the streets but nowhere could he find the blind youth and his beautiful beggar sister. He inquired in the market place and was told that the brother and sister had gone out of the gates of the city seeking a certain prophet who, it was reported, cured the blind and who saved all in distress.

Twice during the past ten days had the brother and sister visited Herodium for this special purpose and each time they failed to find him, although all said that this prophet had recently been in the vicinity.

Rongus gave up his search and returned to the inn. Here he found his master loading the asses.

"Come, we must get along. We cannot remain here."

"I was seeking that blind fellow."

"It is well to learn the streets of any city but it is also good to know the country roads. And we have a great deal of work to do and a good many roads to see."

"But we are only a day's journey from Jerusalem."

"True Rongus, true. But we must learn the other roads also. We must travel the caravan route that goes north to Cæsarea, the great seaport, and we must also see the valley of Sorek and the country directly surrounding Jerusalem. It is many years since I have been in these places and this ground we must know thoroughly, otherwise we are doomed to failure."

"Then we will surely find the blind beggar youth and his sister."

"Come Rongus. Make haste, for we have no time to lose, and tarry is the trap of man."

The leather breast-protector, the brass helmet and the purple toga were in the chariot as the Arab dressed in his own coarse native clothes drove through the arch of the yard. Rongus followed leading the three laden asses. They lost no time in clearing the gates and soon they heard the trumpets behind them. This was the signal for closing the giant doors in the walls of the city. It was sundown.

Every now and again Rongus would look at

39

the weather-beaten Arab in the chariot. He admired his daring. He was happy at the chance that fate had played; happy to be in the open country away from the dusty quarry—away from the Romans. For years his life was laden with toil and now in a single day . . . and all because of the Captain Sulla and an Arab merchant who happened to pass at a critical moment. And he was pleased at the trick they played on the Roman captain. But the chariot and the horses; was that too part of the revenge? Was his master a robber? And was he now slave to an outlaw? These thoughts filled his mind.

They camped in a little grove near the top of the breast-shaped hill where the granite tomb of the great Herod stood. They tied the horses and asses to the trees and before darkness descended upon them they climbed to the top of this mound and examined the tomb. It was completely deserted and overgrown with trees and bushes. No path came anywhere near it and on two sides vines had grown up upon the walls.

The Arab stood contemplating the building. "Here is the spot where I have died a hundred deaths. Here I lived a life of death and here I was doomed. Oh, Herod, Herod, if you were again alive I would now know how best to kill you."

While Rongus walked around the square structure, built of solid masonry without door or window, the Arab stood beside a certain spot in the wall that he knew well and he rested his hand on one of the blocks of granite. His eyes seemed to pierce the stone walls and look inside of the tomb, for he alone knew what it contained.

Later in the evening, when they had descended from the top of the hill, he said to Rongus; "All this brings back to me the days when we worked with mallet and chisel building this resting place for the dead king. I was a prisoner and there were a hundred other prisoners and we knew well that the moment the tomb was finished we would be put to death. Alone I escaped. And during the many years that went between, thirty or more, I have dreamed and planned and schemed all to one end. And now the time has come."

"Master," said Rongus. "If our adventure with the Roman officer is fair sample of your powers

41

then I must admit that nothing in this world is strong enough to resist you."

"Adventure, you say," laughed the Arab. "The Roman was a babe. That was only half an adventure, or even less. A small fraction of a real adventure."

"Well all I can say is, that if you call it but half an adventure then what must a whole adventure be like? The walls of cities must tumble down before you in a real adventure." He looked at him proudly as a boy gazes at his father.

"Yes, the walls and more."

"And whole cities must lay in dust and ruin."

"And when my life was crushed, was there no dust; and is the ruin of a city greater than the ruin of a soul!"

"With all my strength, master, I can accomplish nothing."

"Do not fret Rongus, we will have great need of your strength. And if you will only remain with me this fortnight then I will go before a scribe and in the presence of a clerk I will write you a bill and make you free."

"Oh, master, master. I will serve you well."

"And what will you do when you are free?"

"I will seek out the blind beggar and his sister and tell them that I am not a thief."

"Why?"

"So they may know the truth."

The Arab laughed. "And then, when you have told them this, what then?"

"Then I do not know. Perhaps I will go with them and together we will seek the prophet."

"There are many prophets in Judea. They spring from the wilderness in the night and in the end they return to the dark places from whence they come."

"But people speak of miracles."

"Unless I can see it with my own eyes, Rongus, the miracles are only tricks."

"And there are other reasons too why I would like to find her."

"Because she kissed you?"

"Yes. Because I am a slave and she kissed me and it burns in my heart, and it burns because it is the only act of tenderness that has ever come to me, a slave."

"And your uncle? Will you not go to him once you are free?"

"No. Not even if he were dead would I go to look upon his miserable face."

"I like you, Rongus. I like what you say and I like how you say it. I have made no mistake and even if I had paid your weight in gold I should have done well. I saw you from the first as you lifted up the rock and carried it before the hot-mouthed captain, and I drove the asses purposely into the conflict but I could not for long divert his fury. And then I went on and at every step I felt I must go back; and the farther I went the more set became my wish to have you with me."

"You saved me, master, from a terrible punishment."

"No. I saved you for myself."

They fed their beasts grain from the bags in the packs. And they themselves ate some dates, some strips of dried meat and some cakes stuffed with ground poppy seed. Then they spread a woolen cloth upon the ground and rested.

The sky was now dark. Above them the silvery olive branches swayed in the breeze and in the distance the tall dark cypress trees seemed to fuse the ground with the heavens. A faint breeze perfumed with lemon blew over them but the fruit itself they could not see.

"Yes, Rongus. That is how the world has become. Judea is filled with prophets but these woolly polls are only children of Adam and they puff off their words like so much air. And the Greek traders groan under the load of taxes and the Jews weakened by generations of wars are no longer masters of their own cities. And my own people have been driven so far into the wilderness that we cannot live. In the fertile valleys we find death at the hands of the Roman legions and in the desert there is slow starvation. And the cities that were once the glorious strongholds of Judea are now humble and no one has pride enough to clear away the broken walls. And those who can repair the ruin, will not; and those who would, are in weakness and poverty, and cannot. Who will save Judea!"

"Master, master. If our encounter with the Roman was only a trifle of an adventure then whole cities must fall if you would really put

Goshen College
Library

yourself to it. You master, you alone could save Judea!"

"And that is why I have journeyed far and that is why we camp here tonight. Tomorrow we will enter the tomb of the dead king and take out one or two little things that may prove of value and with these we go on toward Jerusalem."

"And how will we enter this strongly walled room?"

"At daybreak, Rongus, you will see. First I must explain to you what we will find inside. But before I can relate the contents of the tomb, you must know how I came to this place, thirty years ago, and how I concealed myself with the corpse of Herod. . . . And also how I escaped."

IV

"BUT first I must have you know that my name is Barzor. I was born the son of an Arab merchant and we owned a large storehouse that had connected with it granaries and a private bakery. These yards and stores were within the walls of Jerusalem and so large were they that a caravan of a hundred camels could be sheltered for the night. My father was a good man and paid generously for what he received. He employed stable men to look after the feet of the camels and those that were found swollen or bruised were bound in cloths soaked with oil. It mattered not whether the beast belonged to merchant, traveller or thief, the treatment was the same for all. This was the courtesy of the yard. And there were like courtesies in storehouse, granaries and bakery. Nobody left hungry or dissatisfied. And our father brought us up to conduct ourselves with honor and carry our name with pride."

"The name Barzor is still spoken of in Jerusalem. I heard it myself when a boy."

"Yes, Rongus. It was once a name that needed no written bill for the value of a whole city of Judea. But what was once, is no more. My father died in deepest grief and sorrow. All, all was taken from him by that demon Herod. My brother too is dead, and I alone survive and I live only for one aim, one desire.

"And you must also know that I married young and when I married my father established us in the small town of Bethlehem, which is but a short journey away. And the reason for this was the heavy gate taxes that were levied on goods entering Jerusalem. Besides the usual road-money and bridge-money the caravans paid for entering every town on the route and this besides the regular goods taxes and protection money to desert chiefs.

48

All in all, it became unprofitable to carry certain merchandise. But the gate tax at Jerusalem grew very heavy and the corrupt clerks had constantly to be bribed and as much of the merchandise had to be sent elsewhere it was decided that I should receive the goods in Bethlehem. But alas! The happy days I spent with my young wife were all compressed into a single year. At the end of this year a little boy was born to us and on the seventh day of his young life. . . .

"It is all like a shadow and I remember it but dimly. People were coming and going. Some had packed their belongings and fled in the night with their infants in arms. And why? Because of a rumor. Because it was whispered about that three sages had come from the East and had cast certain prophecies, and one of these was that a male child born in Bethlehem would some day become king of Judea. And the people fled, not because they believed this foolishness but for fear of Herod who, sick in heart, believed in all kinds of superstition. And while I knew that he was cruel, cruel to the hilt. . . . He loved his wife but he killed her

49

grandfather Hyrcanus the high priest and he killed her brother too on the very day when he conferred great dignity upon him and gave him the holy vestments of his office; and when this wife grew to hate his love he ordered her slain and upon her innocent blood he added more and more. The two sons that he had with her he also killed for he feared that they might wrest the throne from under him. And old, decrepit and sick with disease he still clung dearly to the throne of Judea. Jealousy consumed his troubled nature and suspecting that his eldest son desired to plot against him, he threw him in prison. And these are only a fraction of the deeds connected with his own family. And outside of his family there were hundreds— whole cities were slain, and his tricks were shrewd and cunning, as when he took hold of the little son of one of the high priests and bit off his ear so, that with blemished body, the boy could never inherit the office of his father. . . . All this I knew too well when I heard of the prophecy cast by the three sages from the East. But I could not believe that. . . . And I laughed at those who fled in the night. But the very next day the soldiers of Herod surrounded the city and entered and slew every boy child, and not one, not one escaped.

"And we hid our child in a basket of old rags and as soon as the soldiers entered I took money, silver and gold, and put it into their pockets and said; 'What you are looking for is not here. The nurse has taken him away—far away.' But the child, innocent of what was going on, cried; and they took up the basket and began to carry it off. I armed myself and made after them but they held me against the wall and then my wife snatched the weapon from my hand and ran it through one of the soldiers. At this the others turned about and a dozen spears pierced her breast. And when she sank to the floor she turned a soft glance upon me and lovingly she whispered; 'This is our end.' She died in my arms.

"As soon as I could collect my senses I set out for Jerusalem. And I reasoned to myself; 'Herod is old. He is seventy. He has ruled long. He is sick with a terrible disease of the bowels and worms already live in the rot of his body. He is half blind. He spends his days consuming his feeble energy with fear, jealousy and mad beliefs. I will go to the booth of an Arab doctor and take his turban and his packages of herbs and I will compound a cure for all his troubles!' This is what I had in my mind and very soon I set to work to carry it out. I dressed myself as a doctor—a new doctor fresh from Eastern lands and went along the streets about the palace walls crying: *I have come from the East and I go to the West; And I carry the herbs that cure the best*.

"Soon Herod's bailiffs came to me and escorted me to the palace and questioned me about my herbs and what skill I had acquired in this profession. I answered everything in proper order. Then they asked me if I could show them the herbs, and this I did willingly, but as they were wrapped in small bits of parchment they had to be opened carefully, and my fingers trembled so that it brought suspicion upon me. Suddenly one of the palace commissioners, standing by, cried out; 'It is Barzor, the son of the merchant!' And when they searched me they found concealed a dagger. 'And is this also,' they asked, 'one of your cures?' Soon the truth was known."

"Oh, master," said Rongus. "Now all was lost."

"Well as you can see I am still alive. But how I lived through those days remains a great wonder. I was at once cast into prison and my father's property and all his possessions were taken away from him and he himself, with his servants and the few sick camels that were given them, driven into the desert. And neither was my elder brother spared. He too and his entire family were driven out of the city. But my father could not bear the hardship of the journey and he died in the desert a broken and a ruined man. I heard this during my first weeks in the prison. My brother lived on for some years until the Roman soldiers arrived with Pilate from Rome and harried the simple desert folk and killed them. My brother was one of those slain. So great was the terror that reigned in Jerusalem at this time that even the learned Rabbi Ezra, eldest son of Joshua the rightful Prince of the Temple, was driven from the gates of the city. And it was all as she said on that fatal night in Bethlehem; 'This is our end.'

"Then I was twenty and now I am fifty-four. Years will dry up the tears but they cannot lift the encrusted ash. Then I was young, as young as you are now. How long ago! And all this time I have spent in training myself for the great events. All these years between were only given over to my apprenticeship. And now the time has come when I will practise my art. Together, Rongus, we will practise the art. And Judea will be freed of both the Romans and the Herods."

"Master," said Rongus. "I knew from the first that my master was no common desert trader. I am secure and thank the Lord for my good fortune."

"And briefly, Rongus, I continue my story. After some weeks in the underground dungeon, expecting death every hour, suddenly some spearmen arrived. 'Now they are come,' I said to myself. 'And the end is here.' They proceeded to walk up and down the long corridors, eating, drinking, making merry, shouting profane words at the air and singing out suddenly for no reason at all. This was a trick and the dying Herod himself must have put them up to it. Suddenly a great commotion started. They began beating each other and with cries and curses pretended to quarrel; they drew their spears and tumbled over one another. Sud-

denly someone cried and gasped. And then there
was silence for a moment. 'They have killed Antipater!' called one of the prisoners. And so it was.
Antipater, the eldest son of Herod, the same who
was cast into prison because of his father's suspicion
and jealousy and was awaiting trial before the
Roman court, he was now dead. And as soon as he
was killed the soldiers, after all the noise and commotion, now departed quietly with heads down,
for even they knew that an evil thing was done.
But still I was alive.

"How long my life was to continue I did not
know. But exactly four days after the spear-men
murdered his son, Herod himself died. And we
heard the echo of joy deep down in the dungeons
beneath the Temple. While in the streets above us
people stopped each other and cried out with glad-
ness; 'Herod is dead!' And there were tears of joy,
and strangers kissed each other in the happiness
of this liberation. But the priests of the Temple,
the evil and corrupt cousins of the dead king came
upon the towers of the Temple and sounded the
trumpets of lamentation. And they proclaimed a
holy grief that nobody felt in his heart. The people,

silenced by this gesture, smiled and went their way.

"But in the palace the wives of the dead king and his children, his spies and his body-guard, the chamberlains and wardens all spoke together in friendship and a final writ was issued, sealed with the cold signet of Herod. It was ordered and proclaimed that every prisoner, nobleman or slave, in the land of Judea should be slain. This would strike at the hearts of thousands of families and give true cause for lamentation, and Judea would be bowed down with grief. The grief due a dead king.

"An old slave belonging to my father, and left behind in the flight, took it upon himself to go to Bethlehem and gather together what remained of my things and possessions. These he sold and, by bribing the jailors, he brought me the gold. When the spear-men arrived for the massacre of the prisoners, they took my gold and chained me to others who were selected to carry the coffin and the funeral chests to the tomb in Herodium. Forty men chained in two rows carried the stone coffin containing the remains of Herod, immersed in

clarified honey. Priests swinging incense burners
and chanting hymns led the way through the
desert and soldiers followed, bearing the shields
and banners of many conquered people. And also
they carried the golden breast-plate presented to
Herod by the great Cæsar himself at the time
when Herod came to Rome and was made king of
the Jews. There were also costly vessels and his
crown, the crown that he took for himself from
the Temple treasure—the old and traditional
crown of the Jews. All these things were carried
in procession. And there were ambassadors and offi-
cials of state from Greece, Babylon, Media and
other far away countries. And there were priests
from Egypt, dressed in their starched linen robes
carrying a clay jar of blessed fragrant spices that
years before had been sent to their cloister in Jerusalem. These spices had been swept together from
the floor when Cleopatra herself was being prepared
for her tomb. They are the crumbs that dropped
from the long linen bandages with which her vo-
luptuous body was carefully wound.

"And there were also priests of other lands carrying holy tributes, each according to his own be-

liefs, to be placed in this tomb. But the heat of the desert warmed the stone of the coffin and the honey swelled up and some of it flowed out from under the lid upon our heads; and thus were we anointed.

"All these things were placed in the temple at Herodium and they were watched over day and night. At the same time we were set to work on the crest of this very hill building the tomb of heavy granite. But as we toiled we knew the reward that awaited us. We knew that the moment all was finished and everything sealed within, according to plan—then, at that moment we were to die. The gold that the spear-men took from me was only for delay; not for my life. This was understood. And I was doubly doomed, for it had been established by custom that no slave working on the tomb of a king should live after the work was completed. But still you see me before you and my life was preserved in the following manner.

"After working many months on the foundation of this little building one of the architects spoke to me. He was a native of Jerusalem and had made plans of many years before for the restoration of the Temple and other places brought to ruin by

Herod's troops. He spoke kindly and seemed to
know my name. After a week or two he took me
aside to help him chalk some lines on several square
granite blocks that he measured and ruled out carefully. One night I was awakened in my sleep. He
stood before me with a finger to his lips indicating
silence. I followed him out of the tent. There in
the moonlight stood a Roman sentinel who was
part of this conspiracy and before him on the
ground three large stones had been thrown out of
the unfinished low wall of the tomb. The soldier
and the architect had pulled them out and they
had nearby three others, the same cubes that I had
helped rule with chalk some time before, but they
were unable to lift them up and set them in place.
Together we set to work and the three stones fitted
the gap perfectly. And I noticed that the difference
between these blocks and the ones that had been
cast out was in the odd shape of the small center
stone. Outside hardly a crack showed and inside
there was half-a-finger space, but the sides that
touched the adjoining blocks were cut in odd
curves and so smoothly did they fit together that
it was not noticeable at all from the outside. Over

the top we sprinkled a little sand. I was ordered to keep my counsel and perhaps I would be rewarded.

"I soon realized what was going on between the soldier and the architect. The center stone was so constructed that it could be rolled out and leave an opening in the wall large enough for a person to squeeze through. It was clear in my mind that they planned to rob the tomb after the body of Herod and the treasures were all set in place. I worked on, encouraged by this stroke of fortune. At the end of a year the structure was done and the eyes of all slaves were raised to heaven with a hollow look of hope.

"Already preparations had been made for leaving this place, and I believe in the morning we were to start, when I was again wakened, this time by the soldier. It was dark but I knew where to go. The architect stood beside the wall and the movable stone was half turned out. They wrenched the chains from my hands but left the iron cuffs on my wrists. 'Remain here. And after two days and all are departed we will return and let you out.' I climbed through the narrow opening and found

60

myself in the dark dank tomb. In another minute they lifted up the stone and groaning under its weight managed to close the opening in the wall. As I told you before, this stone was quite small and it was the large blocks on either side of it that had required my aid.

"Inside all was dark but at the break of day I discovered that one could see a glint of light in several places but hardly a pin could have gone through the cracks. Soon I grew suspicious. Would they really come? Why should they take me out? Was it not better for them that I should perish here with their secret? And so it was. They never came to let me out.

"On the third day, weakened by hunger and depressed by the heavy odor that came from the pungent drugs in Cleopatra's jar and filled the stale air of the tomb, I knew I must save myself. I searched along the wall and, by the shape of the block and that little crevice that was half-a-finger wide, I soon located the stone and though I pressed with all the strength that remained in me, it did not budge. I tried again and again and when my strength was exhausted I sat down and rested

61

until I could try again. At length after several hours' work I discovered that the edge had to be pressed upward. This was easy enough once one learned the secret and the stone fell to the ground. My heart beat quickly. I hung my head out of the opening, breathing in the fresh night air until I was sufficiently revived to squeeze myself through.

"Once outside, I realized that all was safe. The camp had been moved and there was nobody to be seen. I thought of the holy crown of the Jews and the golden breast-plate and the other treasures that were inside but I feared going back, and having managed to save my life, regarded all else as trifling. I put the stone back in its place and came cautiously down the hill. There was not a soul to be seen and as I was famished I climbed a date tree and ate huge handfuls of the fruit. Then I went on. One thing I knew and that was that I must keep clear of the cities and make my way into the wilderness. At night I walked toward the east and when I saw daylight approaching I hid myself in caves or between rocks and slept a wink or two, but always with my ear to the ground.

In about a week I was already far into the desert. At last I was free!"

Rongus took his master's hand. "Oh master, master," he said. "I have been a slave in a quarry myself but I have never suffered a fraction of what you must have endured. From the day my uncle sold me to the day you took me away I had never experienced anything except the whip."

"And now, Rongus, it is late and we should be asleep but I must conclude my adventure in order that you may fully understand what we are about. Some years later I learned that the architect and the soldier quarrelled and in the heat of the argument the soldier was killed and the architect fled into the desert. I saw him myself and he told me the story from his own lips. But I was no longer a slave and he begged for mercy on his knees before me. And to this very day the tomb has never been entered.

"I must also tell you that after I left the tomb and was travelling for several weeks, I was one day surrounded by a band of robbers and taken to their chief who turned out to be the great Hezekias. And as I stood in his tent before him I laughed. I

laughed full in his face. And then I said to him;
'Loose the cords that tie me and I will tell you why
I laugh.'

"Then I related truthfully everything that happened to me from the time when the three sages,
who came out of the East, cast forth their prophecies. And I ended by saying that nothing could
suit me better than being captured by an Arab
band, for then I was safe from the Romans and
also from the spies of Herod's palace. Then I told
him my name and he came down from his couch
and took me in his arms. He unbuckled his belt
and sword and put them on me saying; 'This for
the memory of your father and with all things it
will be likewise as though you were my own son.'
And from that moment my education began. I
learned what was real and false, what was brave
and what was mean. I learned the life of the desert.
And in time I became the chief lieutenant of Hezekias and everything he knew he taught me. And
I was already in this position when the architect
who killed the soldier was brought before me. He
told me the story of the quarrel and begged for his
life; 'As I have saved you, reward that kindness

and let me go.' Then I said to him; 'I was a slave and I aided you with a deed of trickery. I did this to save my life. But you, fearing that while I lived the secret of your evil scheme might become known. . . . Yes, you saved me and wrenched the chains from my arms but only to entomb me alive. You thought it was impossible to move the stone from the inside but I did and here I am. And you who wanted my death will now be rewarded in the coin of your ambition. I am now a different person, unlike the one you pretended to have saved. Then I looked upon the world as a place of love, of pity, of kindness, of mercy. Here was brother and brother, father and son and mother and daughter. But it's false! As false as you are yourself. The world is force and strife! Man is a deceiver; he lives in discord with his brothers and in a broil with himself; he acts with cunning and he mounts to the high places only by sly tricks, falsehood and roguery. And you my good architect; what you promised to give to others and refused, that very thing will now be taken away from you.'

"When he heard these words he knew he was lost. 'I will divide with you,' he cried. 'Everything will be divided between you and me.' I smiled. 'Why should I give you half, if I can take the whole?' I reasoned. 'But it's my plan, my device, my risk, my everything.' Then I answered him softly and said; 'And it was your plan also, to leave me dead in the tomb!'

"And once more he pleaded. But I cut him short and said; 'You must die. We do not need the treasure in the tomb. But you must die because your word has been broken and what you have broken before you may break again.' Then I gave the signal and he was killed. And as he was dying I watched him closely. I forced my eyes to look upon this brutal thing saying to myself; 'Look at it Barzor, that you may see that there is only one stroke between life and death. Watch him closely so that your heart may accustom itself to this agony, that the thing called mercy may be wrung from the tissues of your body. For he is the first and many more must follow. Judea! Judea! It has come to this and from now on this must be my life.'"

"Oh, master, master," cried Rongus. "Now I know everything and I understand."

"In the years that followed we engaged upon many adventures and all together they have been to me only an apprenticeship. Now the good chief Hezekias is dead and I am free to lead our men into Jerusalem itself. But first the ground must be prepared. We must know how the land is arranged and what is the strength and temper of the Roman legions. We must know everything before we bend the bow for the shot. We face great odds and openly we can do nothing. It is for that reason that you see me dressed as an Arab merchant. So, avoiding the main roads, I came upon the Roman quarry. I looked down from above and saw everything that was going on. Then I drove the asses down the rocks and between the Roman captain and yourself.

"Now we must sleep for at dawn we will try our hand at the stone in the wall of the tomb and if we succeed in moving it, the crown of the Jews will be restored to its rightful place in the Temple and the money-snatching priests and all the black cousins of Herod will be driven out."

"Master, no matter what happens, I will serve you truly and faithfully."

"And everything I have told you Rongus is the truth. But you must forget that my name is Barzor. It was written in the desert sand and the winds have rubbed it out."

"Not a word of anything you have told me will ever pass my lips."

"And now we sleep."

Rongus fatigued by the freedom of his new life quickly closed his eyes and for the moment before he fell asleep he thought of his master sealed within the tomb and he also brought to his mind the image of the beautiful girl, the sister of the blind beggar. He imagined her soft arms still entwined about his neck. And to himself he whispered; 'I will seek her out. I will find her.' And with these words on his lips he fell asleep.

V

At daybreak Barzor awoke Rongus. They had first to look after the animals. One of the asses had broken his rope and wandered down the hill, probably seeking water. He was brought back and tied up securely. After eating a bite of bread and part of a small dried fish they climbed to the top of the hill and set to work.

The stone did not look as though it would move at all. The wind had driven a dust of many years into the cracks, but with a small bit of metal and considerable patience they scraped it clean. Soon it began to loosen and as they worked it back and forth a sprinkling of dry sand fell from the crevices. As soon as the stone was worked out a small distance slight grooves on the sides presented themselves and these enabled one to take hold more firmly. Now, it rotated, first to one side and then to the other, and at last fell to the ground.

Rongus brushed the sand away from the opening and the Arab climbed through the hole.

Once inside, he spoke; "It's very dark in here, Rongus. I had better wait a minute or two until my eyes begin to see some of the things. You remain where you are and I will pass out what we want. And keep one eye on the lookout for Roman sentinels. Should one appear, climb inside and we will be safe. If the opening is discovered and they attempt to come inside, they must do so one by one, and as they enter we will kill them. But I don't think we'll have to."

"Can you see better now?" asked the slave anxiously. "Are the things all there?"

"Yes, I can see better and I smell the Cleopatra spices. But the golden breast-plate should be on this side and it is not. . . ." He stumbled but caught himself. "Here it is. The straps have rotted away

70

and it fell to the ground." He brought it to the hole in the wall and handed it out to Rongus.

The breast-plate was tarnished and black but it was heavy and had the feel of good gold. It was, besides, a beautiful thing and Rongus measured it with his eye. Was it small or too large? Would it fit him? Would his master allow him to wear it once—just once? And Sulla's leather corslet studded with brass nails, what did it look like compared to the proud armor of a king! He examined the straps. They were green with mold and crumbling with decay. The buckles were encrusted with a corroding salt and would have to be scraped.

"Where are you, Rongus?" came a call from inside.

"Here. Here."

"Take this. But be careful!"

Out came Cleopatra's jar of spices. It was as small as a dog's head and made of dull red clay with a lid tied in place with a hard twisted grass that had been dipped in melted rosin. It felt cold as ice when Rongus laid his hands on it and brought

71

it out into the light, and a heavy aroma seemed to seep through its porous clay.

"Everything is in its place," said the Arab. "The architect told the truth when he said that nobody has learned his secret. Everything is here."

He groped about in the dark while Rongus watched cautiously at the entrance.

"Here is the crown!"

Rongus took hold of the tarnished metal band and examined it carefully. In the meantime Barzor pulled himself through the narrow opening and seemed much relieved when he was out in the open. He cast a quick glance about him to see that they were not being watched and then together they replaced the stone.

After this was accomplished Barzor broke a small branch from a brush and swept away the footprints that they had made standing beside the wall. Then quickly they departed.

The objects taken from the tomb were wrapped carefully and concealed in the packs.

Rongus spoke and said; "The straps on the golden armor are rotted away."

72

"Yes. I have noticed."

"We could cut new straps from the horses' harness."

"Yes. But we must not stop now. Sulla may have raised the alarm and Herodium will be far from safe. The chariot cannot easily be hidden from sight. Let's hurry."

They loaded the asses and fixing the horses in place beside the long shaft of the chariot set out across the rough, barren ground until they struck the highway that would take them towards Jerusalem by way of Bethlehem. This was a less frequented road than the one they travelled the day before with the Roman, Sulla.

The Arab rode slowly behind in the chariot while Rongus drove the asses before him. They stopped at a watering place and, first making certain that the water was not poisoned, they filled the empty skins. These were tied in pairs and hung on the beasts' shoulders. The cool sides of the water skins offered a slight protection from the burning sun. But their dampness attracted pesky swarms of flies. The asses, however, recognized the fresh water next to their packs and jogged on with greater as-

73

surance. Even the beasts in this land know that thirst is the great demon of the desert.

At noon they found cool shade beside a group of fragrant lemon trees, and rested.

Rongus spoke; "I could clean the breast-plate with some of these lemon leaves."

"It's not worth the trouble. We can sell it as it is."

"Master; the golden breast-plate is a beautiful thing. It would be a pity to sell it."

"What good is it to us?"

"It is a proud thing and perhaps you would let me wear it once. If we find the sister of the blind boy I could put it on and then she would know that I spoke the truth."

Barzor laughed.

"Yes. I could put it on for protection also. For one reason or another it might prove useful."

"You may take Sulla's leather corslet for protection."

"Oh master! How can you compare a bit of soiled leather with. . . . Truly master, it would be a pity."

"But we need coined gold and silver and that

is why I took it from the tomb. We should have taken some other objects if this were not to be sold."

"We can go back, master."

"No. There is little time to be lost. We must work quickly for we still have much ground to cover. If your heart is set on the golden breast-plate we may sell some other things that are in the packs. But back we cannot go. Will the breast-plate fit you?"

"Perfectly master. I am sure."

Rongus quickly untied the bundle containing this precious object, and to prove to his master that it was not too small or too large, he tried it on.

"See master. It lies snug like the scales on a fish."

Barzor smiled. He could see that the youth was fascinated by the golden breast-plate. His whole spirit seemed changed. His eye took on a proud glance and his whole carriage had an upright grace and assurance.

"Really it does fit," said the Arab. "And I would give it to you for your own if only I did not fear that it would attract undue attention and bring trouble upon us."

"Master, I could attach new straps and polish it nicely and then wear it underneath."

"Underneath?"

"Yes. Under my shirt."

"Then nobody could see it."

"That would not matter. We would know it was there, and all the time, wherever we went I could feel it and this would give me courage. And with courage I could laugh in the face of Roman archers and play tricks with a whole troop of spear-men."

"If you promise to keep it well hidden you may have it for yourself."

"I promise master. Oh, it is wonderful, truly wonderful."

He broke some small branches of lemon twigs and stripping off a handful of the leaves, he crushed them into a ball and began rubbing the metal, first inside and then without. It soon began to glisten. The Arab in the meantime found some strips of leather in one of the packs and after making holes that would attach to the buckles and cutting them to the proper length, he put it on Rongus and fastened it securely. Over it Rongus closed his shirt, and over his shirt he threw the tattered and patched woolen rag that he called his cloak.

Now he smiled. "Master, never will I leave you. If only I could see my uncle now, I could open my shirt and say; 'See, you old money-louse! This alone is worth more than all the clipped and sweated coins in your bags.'"

"Has he so much?"

"He changes money by the piece or by the weight. He makes a commerce in coins."

"In Jerusalem?"

"Yes."

"Perhaps we can find him and perhaps we can sell him what we have and receive from him the coins we require."

"He will only cheat you, master. He is a fox and I must warn you."

The Arab laughed so hard that he had to hold his sides. "He will cheat us, you say!" And he laughed some more. "Oh, Rongus, you are a pleasure and a delight. Why should he cheat us?"

"Because I know the old wretch and I warn you. He clips his coins and when they are weighed he holds the balance with a twisting finger. I must warn you."

"But really, Rongus. Why should he cheat us when we can more easily cheat him?"

"Oh, master, forgive me. I forgot. He is such a fox I did not think anyone could cope with him. What wouldn't I give to see the old money-grubber get his due! Oh, master, I would kiss the dust between your feet."

"Then it is settled. We will go to him and you can demand the money that he received from the Romans when he sold you into bondage. We will invent some pretext. But first we must stop in Bethlehem and put away the horses and the chariot. Come."

This highway that stretched north to Bethlehem and Jerusalem had fallen into a state of neglect. Here and there drifts of sand blown by desert winds covered parts of the road, the narrow wheels of the chariot sank deep and the hoofs of the horses buried themselves in the loose ground. The loaded asses however made fair headway over the bad parts of the road. But Rongus had to keep his stick in hand and prevent the beasts from grazing on the young thorn bushes that had recently grown up at the sides of the road. Because of the sweet juices, the foolish animals, if left to themselves, would chew this hostile plant until their mouths bled.

At the crest of the hill a low sandstone breach in the land sheltered them from the burning sun. They paused to survey the low hills before them. Here and there drifts of crumbled pumice bleached by the sun stood out from the clusters of broken blocks of dark lava and jagged black stones. The rising heat far in the distance was quite noticeable for the columns of warm air moving upward from the hot sands distorted the view of the far away hills which seemed to sway like waves in a sea.

Directly beneath them in a fairly fertile valley stood Bethlehem. The dark walls seemed low from this height and the white marble of its temple and small arena glistened in the sun.

Faintly in the distance they could also see the black tops of the towers of Jerusalem. These squares of stone seemed to press down the light colored, loose ground beneath them as though the whole city had sunk away into a sinister quicksand.

They wiped the fine grains from the corners of their eyes, moistened their sun-dried lashes with a stroke of a finger and drove on. Downhill they travelled rapidly and were soon at the gates of the city. Here the Arab paid toll to one collector at the gate and gave a handful of silver to another who was stationed to examine all merchandise passing into the city.

"We have nothing, brother, but we must make haste," he said handing him the silver.

The collector weighed it in his hand and said quietly; "Pass on."

Behind the inner doors of the wall were long rows of olive wood posts driven into the ground. Here beasts of burden were tied. Here the Arab left Rongus with the horses and asses while he went with rapid steps to the market place.

An old Arab with skin almost black and white hair and beard sat before a basket of carefully folded clothes and beside him was an open box containing rough blocks and strings of clear amber.

80

He had come from somewhere in the desert several weeks before, and day after day, although he sold nothing, he took his place in the market square beside the perfumers' booths.

As soon as he caught sight of Barzor from the corner of his eye he closed down the lid of his box with a bang and taking up the large basket of stuffs cried out, as though in anger; "The devil take it! Nobody will buy. Fine stuffs from India and amber clear as honey and I must wear my cloak thin sitting here all day. The devil take it!"

The Jewish merchants in the perfumery booths laughed at the impatience of the departing Arab. But they did not notice that when he left the market place Barzor followed close upon his heels and to lighten the burden he carried the box of amber. The two Arabs did not say a word to each other. The older man led the way and Barzor followed.

Soon they came to a house surrounded by a low wall, and here they entered the gate. Once in the yard and the wooden door closed behind them, the old man stopped. "This is the house I have hired."

"Very good, Yaba," said Barzor. "It will suit us perfectly."

"The yard is small."

"No matter. It will do."

"And the camels?"

"The two I brought with me I have given out to pasture so that they may be rested and well fed. The boy brings them back at sundown and we tie them up here inside the yard."

"Good. And the other things?"

"Everything is in the house and the black slave watches while I am away."

"And in the market place? What goes on, Yaba?"

"Nothing. There is no money and there is no food. Dark days have fallen upon Judea and the people fear that Pilate will send his soldiers to tax the fruit within the walls of Bethlehem as he has recently done in Jerusalem."

"Good. Let him tax every hair on their heads! And on the road what is the news?"

"Everything in order. Three caravans have left Jerusalem in a single week. Two have gone north toward upper Galilee and one will head northwest for Cæsarea."

"And what is coming toward Jerusalem?"

"Light caravans are reported, of which two are

heavily guarded. The rich Alexandrian merchant is sending another golden tribute to the Temple and there are besides forty camels in his train loaded with beans and gourds from Egypt and Greece and wine from Rome. Two beasts are also piled high with Egyptian baskets. The rich Jew himself is probably still in Cæsarea."

"Wine from Rome?"

"Yes, Barzor. The soldiers are complaining. They do not like the native fruit vinegar and our wine is costly for their purses. It had been ordered last year, and more is coming by land with the second guarded caravan. This contains fifty camels and brings the annual silver tribute from the Jews in Rome to their holy Temple. The captain carries a parchment roll from the Emperor and the entire caravan may pass anywhere tax free."

"How far away are they?"

"Six days still. Perhaps five. They are pushing hard to arrive with the tribute before the holy days."

"Well that meets with our plans splendidly. And the other six caravans?"

"They are unguarded. But all have paid protection money. They carry the usual merchandise, salt from the Dead Sea, plates from Babylon, household vessels from Sidon. There is good trade in these, for, as you know, tradition dictates that each household should have new utensils at this season."

"What else, Yaba? What more is coming?"

"The usual. Sandals from Laodicea, shirts from Cilicia, dresses from India, veils from Arabia, dried fish from Spain, apples from Crete, more lentils, more beans, more gourds, all from Greece and the islands brought overland through Egypt, cheese from Bithynia but no beer from Media. Not a single skin."

"No beer?"

"Something went wrong in the making this year and the skins all burst after three days of desert heat."

Barzor laughed. "And Ben Rashid the Alexandrian merchant you say is still in Cæsarea?"

"He is pious and means to leave soon for Jerusalem where he has an honored place in the Temple during the Passover Services. But the three sons

of the old Rabbi Ezra are secretly working in Jerusalem."

"Good. And the fair Greek girls?"

"Everything is in order. They are weary of the
old Alexandrian Jew and are in mood for anything. The chief black eunuch is friendly. But the
whole city of Cæsarea, dependent on this wealthy
merchant for the few pennies that, from time to
time, he gives away with magnanimous gestures,
watches closely to defend his property and inter-
ests. The whole city is armed in his defense."

"Let them watch as close as they may," said
Barzor. "Tonight we set out for Cæsarea. But first
we must hurry to Jerusalem. Listen carefully, Yaba.
Send your black to the south gate and let him
bring the asses and the chariot and the young Hebrew slave that I have bought."

"You bought a Hebrew slave! You know what
is said: 'He who buys a Hebrew slave buys a master
for himself.'"

"Wait until you see him. Let them come at once.
Then while we change our clothes, let him hire
two fresh asses for we must leave within the hour

for Jerusalem. Then as soon as we are gone bring in the camels from their pasture, have them properly bridled and mounted each with a curtained litter. In the leather bags place some sugared fruit and a small pouch of liquorice bark and salted nuts. The white Greek girls will need some encouragement. And have the two mounted camels outside the walls at sundown so that we can start as soon as we return from Jerusalem with the money."

Yaba called the black slave and sent him running on his first errand. Then he said to Barzor; "I will make myself ready."

"No Yaba. I forgot to tell you that I will take the young Hebrew slave with me and you will remain here in case more information arrives. You understand these affairs better than anyone. Only one thing more, I neglected to ask you about our men."

"All are safe and everything is according to plan."

"They know that they must not rob any caravans or merchants?"

"Yes."

"And they must not molest pious travellers coming to Jerusalem for the Temple services?"

"Yes. They do not like to see so much pass them by. They sit uneasy in their saddles but we have promised them greater spoils and they are now encamped at the distance we have set. They await our signals patiently."

VI

■■

WHEN the packs were unloaded and everything
including the chariot was safe in the yard, Barzor
entered the house and gave Rongus fresh linen and
a robe of costly stuff. He also gave him leather
sandals, a silver dagger and he wound about his
head a turban of fine white silk. Underneath his
cloak was the golden breast-plate. Then he examined him from head to foot and seemed pleased.

Before the black slave could return with the two
fresh asses for the short journey to Jerusalem, Barzor had also changed his attire completely. Arriving in Bethlehem they had looked like two miserable desert wanderers; a poor trader, too poor to

pay the protection money necessary to join a well equipped caravan, and with him his ragged boy. But when they departed they looked like princes of rich and vast Arabian domains. In a small bag they carried plates of gold and other costly object set with precious stones. These were to be sold or silver and gold coin.

The animals ran along at a lively pace ere the road was in excellent repair and along the sides were occasional wanderers going Jerusalem on foot. The travellers carried sacs of dried fruits and other native products that could be sold in the crowded city or exchanged for meats and the unleavened bread required at this season.

They passed several fresh water wells but these were covered over with thorn-bush to indicate that the water was not good to drink. Two water peddlers in Jerusalem had recently been stoned to death because they had poisoned the water of a nearby well; and this was done so that travellers in this part would all be required to purchase the few drops of water necessary to quench their thirst. But these were scapegoats, and forty or more water peddlers were not discovered and most of the desert wells about the city walls were polluted, so that this filthy crew of peddlers could enrich their trade with their cry: "Fresh and good, clear and sweet, worth a fortune and only a penny a cup!" The few good public watering places were guarded night and day by Roman soldiers.

Several chariots driven by Roman officers passed them on the road and made room for the travellers so splendidly dressed. Had Sulla himself driven by he would certainly not have recognized them.

Barzor and Rongus rode on. The land had suddenly become quite fertile and here and there farmers in the fields were already cutting the golden wheat and ripe corn. In this part of the world the harvest takes place in the early spring of the year.

At one roadside farmhouse the threshing was already in progress. A poor underfed Egyptian slave drove an ox round and round. "Thresh for yourself, thresh for yourself, you miserable ox!" cried the slave. "Thresh for yourself! Straw for your fodder; corn for your master; give yourself no peace!" He repeated these lines with sing-song voice, over and over.

Now Barzor said to Rongus as they were arriving at the walls of the city; "We may not tarry long and whatever is to be done must be accomplished quickly."

The large wooden gates that had once been covered with plates of gold and were the glory of the East, now hung in a dilapidated state. The wood was old and rotted. The holes which had once contained the bolts for securing the precious metal had not been filled and many of the black wooden pegs fastening the oak sections together were gone. One of the doors, sagging badly, had been trussed up with a cross beam and both had crude bronze plates attached to the bottom to keep out rats and scorpions. The stone door-sills had recently been repaired and they contained iron rings to which the closed doors could be chained. Beggars, lame, blind, scurvy, diseased and ulcerated, cried out in chorus at the arrival of even the most humble traveller. But when someone arrived richly dressed their voices rose still louder, insistent and quite threatening.

In several places the walls of the city lay low in ruins. These gaps had been filled by the splin-

tered beams of catapults and other crude engines
of war. A wild brush and young trees had taken
root in these rough openings. It seemed strange
that the heavy timbers once used as battering-
rams to crumble the stones of the walls should now
fill the breach of their own destroying. The many
years that had followed the siege had not found
in the city spirit or pride enough to repair that
solid front of masonry, once the mighty and glorious stronghold of the entire land. That spirit and
pride, at one time all powerful, was now crushed
under the ruins never to rise again.

What was true of the walls of the city was also
true of the interior. The inner walls that enclosed
a large section of the Temple were in no better condition except in the few places where repairs had
been attempted. But the Temple and surrounding
palaces had all been rebuilt and sections of these
buildings were, even at this date, being enlarged
and repaired. All else in the city seemed in miserable condition and that which was not already
complete ruins seemed tottering and about to fall.

The large open courts before the Temple presented a busy and colorful sight. The greater part

of this space was devoted to an animal mart. Here
natives of outlying districts would bring their
sheep and oxen to be sold to the Temple priests.
Here also the animals were fed, cleaned and prepared for slaughter. Besides the customary sacrifice depending upon the season, two lambs and one
ox were selected daily to be placed on the altar as
a tribute to the Emperor of Rome. These fattened
animals were separated from the rest and kept in
special pens. The whole section was guarded by
Temple bailiffs who carried knives in their belts
lest a hungry crew of beggars should attempt to
steal a lamb from one of the enclosures.

At the far end of the court were the long tiers
of boxes for pigeon breeding. These birds were
killed with special rites and ceremony and sold to
the public who placed them on the altar of sacrifice.

To get to the money changers' tables Barzor and
Rongus had to cross the mud and filth in the lane
between the animal stalls. They raised their silken
robes and stepped gingerly over the bad places.
The tables, some with cloth canopies set at an an-

gle to give shelter from the heat of the sun, stood along a low wall near the main gate. Here Barzor read the inscription cut in the stone: "No stranger may enter within the balustrade about the Temple and its enclosure. The guilty are liable to a punishment of death." Arabs, Greeks and Romans were all strangers. The inner courts were reserved for Jews and the inner shrines, of which there were many, for the high priests alone.

Rongus kept his eyes sharpened. He glanced rapidly along the lines of beggars to see if he could discover the blind boy and his sister. But nowhere did he see them. Then he searched about until he found the booth of his uncle.

The money changer did not recognize his nephew as the two paused before him. The merchandise was unwrapped and placed on the table. The rate of exchange was established between them. Pure gold brought twelve times its weight in silver coins. The money changer weighed each piece with great care and he was happy at this fine bit of business that had suddenly fallen to his lot. He said; "And you need all the coin at once?"

"Yes. Immediately," Barzor replied.

"Then I must borrow from one of my colleagues."

He beckoned with his finger and called into partnership one of his corrupt cousins and together they helped fill nine heavy bags with large silver coins and two small bags with gold.

The business seemed complete. Barzor and Rongus made several trips to the court gate and, securing the money in the packs which were guarded by two court-yard bailiffs, returned for a last bag. Pesky beggars cried aloud for a single penny.

"I hope you fine gentlemen will come again," said the changer of coin.

"If it pleases my master," Barzor replied, "we will be here often."

"Your master?" said the astonished merchant. "You are only a servant? And dressed in silk and. . . ."

"My master is young and handsome and princes of the blood could well be his servants. He stands before you." With these words Barzor pointed to Rongus who stood behind him erect and with a proud tilt to his head.

The merchant bowed low with respect. And as

Rongus nodded his reply he opened the neck of his shirt slightly to show a gleam of the golden breast-plate underneath.

"Uncle. You do not seem to recognize me?"

The merchant rubbed his eyes.

"Have you forgotten the little son of your brother?"

"Oh Rongus! My boy Rongus! Can I believe my eyes! What a happy day has befallen us!" His arms were outstretched but Rongus did not step forward to meet his uncle's embrace.

Now Barzor stepped between them. "It is forbidden," he said, "to come within arm's length of the prince."

"The prince!" cried the merchant. "My nephew a prince!"

"No prince of Arabia is so rich as my master, nor so generous. But it is forbidden—he has powerful enemies—to come closer."

"Oh Rongus. I knew it. Always I dreamed that some day you would thus appear before me. And the long nights that I lay awake thinking and hoping and praying for your safety. And now my prayers have been answered, and indeed the Lord is merciful."

"Uncle, I stand now before you and there are seven years buried between us. If I have prospered, I hope you have also prospered."

"Yes. Things have gone a little better with me."

"That is good. For I must tell you that besides being a prince of Arabia and ruling over lands that are vast, I am also protector of the Persian caravans and they pay tribute to me in silver and in gold."

"My own little Rongus."

"And besides the routes to Persia we have our own caravans that go each year to upper Egypt and I am here now to meet them on their return. ... And for another purpose too, Uncle!" he placed his hand on his dagger. "I am here to plan your ruin. What you have sold you must now buy back. I want the money you received from the Romans. Two-hundred pieces of silver was the price you sold me for. On your knees, you black son of a dog! Or I will cry out so all may hear that you sold me, the child of your dead brother, and now that I am the richest prince of all Arabia, the whole

97

Temple court will laugh you into your grave. And what they cannot accomplish by jest, my forty men from the desert will complete. They may begin by digging your grave. Two-hundred pieces of silver! And on your knees!"

The frightened merchant was now trembling. "I meant you no wrong. I want peace only. . . . Only peace."

"On your knees!"

He took a bag of silver in his shaking hands; "May all present bear witness that I now return to the son of my brother the money that . . ." Words failed him. His knees sank to the ground.

At that moment Barzor cried out; "Beggars of ill fortune. Come! The silver is for you!" And saying this he tore open the bag and scattered the coins far and wide on the pavement along the changers' booths.

There was a great outcry and a mad scramble. The lame, the maimed and even the blind rushed in and snatched from the ground and from each others' hands. The merchants cried out and quickly lifted their bags of money into safety on the wall. But some were not quick enough and in the mad

scramble for the silver coins, several of the bles
were upset and the loose money thus scattered ly
renewed the fight between the beggars. At last th
blind were on their knees brushing the pavement
rapidly with their hands for a stray coin. They
crept everywhere under the tables and the merchants kicked them brutally to drive them off lest
the flimsy boards of their booths be wrecked.

Barzor and Rongus were already quietly on their
way when the Temple bailiffs ran into the court
to establish order. As all the money on the ground
had quickly been snatched up the beggars departed
quarrelling among themselves. And now merchants
with cry and gesture, with curses and in heated
anger, argued, shouted, lamented and called lustily
upon the Lord. The miserable uncle became the
center of the storm of reproach, but as he was on
his knees when it all happened and could save none
of the loose coins from his overturned table, and
as his cries for his own ruin were louder than the
cries of all the rest, they left him soon to argue
among themselves.

Once outside the tumbling gates of the city, Barzor and Rongus mounted the asses and kicking them smartly, set off at a brisk gait.

"Goodbye Jerusalem," laughed Barzor. "We will see you again."

VII

THEY pushed the animals hard and kept them trotting most of the way. But the sun had already gone behind the low gravel hills in the distance and the trumpets had sounded from the gates of Bethlehem. The heavy doors were closed for the night when they reached the city.

The old Arab Yaba and his black slave were at the appointed place outside the walls. Beside them kneeled two large camels mounted with curtained litters. These woolly beasts of the desert swung their long necks from side to side and chewed an everlasting cud.

Yaba spoke; "The palace of the Jew has three

101

turrets facing the sea. The door to the walled garden is on the north side. And the name of the chief
_ _k eunuch is Zozo. His bones are large and the
gola , in about his neck is made of twisted links.
You will . o know him by a broken tooth which
shows plainly in his mouth. For a little gold he
would sell his father and his mother. The girls have
a pure white skin that has never been uncovered
to the sun. They are weary of the old Jew. But
the palace is protected by an armed guard and there
are also many retainers ready to defend the property of their lord—even to a bunch of grapes. They
are desperate cutters."

The bags of money were secured in the litters
and covered over with small sacks of provisions
and several skins of water. When all was ready,
Barzor and Rongus mounted and the old Arab
yanking the camels by their beards awoke them
from their drowsiness and in another moment they
were up and off.

They cut across the road that had brought them
to Bethlehem and turned towards the sinking sun.

"Master! Master!" called Rongus. "Only for a
moment, but I must turn back. We will be gone

for some days and I must say something to Yaba."

Barzor halted. Rongus turned about and the old Arab came forward to meet him.

"While we are gone you might be on the lookout for a blind beggar boy."

"There are many such."

"You will know him. He carries an iron rod with small clanking rings and his sister leads him. She is fair and seeks some prophet who performs miracles."

"I am an old man and I have seen much and there is much that I have not seen. But this I know: The miracles are only sorcery."

"No matter. While we are gone, if you see such a pair, do me the service and have them wait until we return."

With these words he turned sharply about and, jabbing the camel-stick into the neck of the loose-jointed beast, soon caught up with Barzor.

It had been a long and eventful day and not even the bracing cool air of the evening was sufficient to refresh their weariness. But they were carrying a valuable cargo and riding on a mission that could daunt the pride of the bravest; they dare not stop nor linger. These tremblers in the field must not be overcome by the soft kiss of sleep.

Rongus swayed limply from side to side with the tossing about of the soft-footed desert beast who swished back a throw of sand with each step. It had been years since he had ridden a camel and he was unaccustomed to the heaving and twisting motion. His mind was filled with the adventures of the past few days. So much had happened that he almost forgot where it all began. He almost forgot the quarry and the Roman bully, Sulla.

He felt his arms, he pressed his hands together, his fingers touched his dagger and his hand went inside his cloak and over the smooth polished gold of the breast-plate. The breast-plate of an emperor! It was all real. This was no dream of a desert peddler and the merchandise contained no combs for soft beards. Here was a traffic without barter in a currency of wits, minted with cunning and stamped with a blow direct and daring. Once again he vowed he would never leave his wonderful master.

As night closed upon them Barzor watched the sky before him so that he could set the course by

the stars, for soon the distant gap in the hill that
guided him would be reached. One by one the stars
pricked their pin-pointed places in the heavy blue
above them. On they went. They forced through
steadily. When they saw the dawn approaching,
they brought their camels to a kneeling position
and tying their forelegs together with a bit of
rope they stretched out in the sand beside the animals and fell asleep.

They reached Cæsarea the following afternoon
and made straight for the market place. Zozo, the
black eunuch, tall and erect, with bright red turban and a heavy golden chain of twisted links about
his neck, was walking about the stalls and booths.

"You are expecting us," said Barzor.

The negro laughed. His broken tooth showed
plainly. "Perhaps you, or perhaps someone else."

"We are the ones."

"How should I know?"

"Come, we will talk."

The negro followed them out of the market
place to a secluded spot by the wall of the city.

"Say, what is it you want?" asked the negro.

"The Greek girls."

"Impossible."

"We want all three."

"Impossible."

"Won't they come willingly?"

"Yes. That they would do. Their kind are ready for anything. But they are closely watched. We are all watched."

"Well, as long as they are willing, we will manage it."

"But they want to go home to the land of their birth and they have offered me a fine reward if I could help them."

"Say to them that two rich merchants are ready to conduct them to the governor of Judea and he will hear them and give them justice."

"But then I would get no reward."

"There will be a hundred pieces of gold for you."

"A hundred pieces! Each girl would bring five-hundred in any market. And where would I be? I could not remain here. And if they found me and brought me back they would break my bones with a stick and not even two-hundred pieces of gold could buy them off."

"But yourself, you cannot sell them."

"I know, that is true. But their worth is great nevertheless."

"For yourself you need have no concern. We will take you with us and they will never find you. And the girls knowing that you will journey with them to Jerusalem will leave anxiety behind."

"I can manage the girls sometimes, but sometimes all the gods in heaven could not manage them. The risk is great."

"What risk?"

"The walls of the palace are guarded day and night. And armed men watch lurking in each tower."

"But the Jew. Where is he now?"

"He has gone with one of his caravans. He may return at any moment. One never knows when he comes or goes. But his men are desperates and ribalds. If they went back to the sea where they came from they would be a crew that would rival the greatest of pirates. The Jew pays them well; they eat plenty and are ever ready to prove their worth."

"And you yourself?"

"I am without manhood and being without . . .
The men laugh at me and the women in the harem
torture me with their cuckolding and cozzying
tricks. For want of better they give me no rest
and if I did not beat them they would kiss me
until the breath were out of my body. So you see
I am ready for anything honorable but a hundred
pieces is too little."

"Two-hundred!"

"Give it to me now."

"No. Not until the girls are in the litters."

"How then can I show to them that you are not
a common desert peddler?"

"You will have one hundred now and the rest
in the morning."

"But the walls are narrowly watched and it may
not be possible."

"Let them watch as close as they may. Have the
girls ready at the break of dawn. Station yourself
by the door in the garden wall and we will drive
by—and off we go."

He paid the black a hundred pieces of gold.

"But one thing make certain. No matter what

happens, do not leave the Greek girls alone. And no matter what goes on along the beach, do not go far from the garden door. Not even so much as a dozen paces."

VIII

DIRECTLY the eunuch had gone, Barzor sent Rongus back to the market place to buy a large jar of oil and as soon as he returned with it they set out to find a place along the fertile coast where they could give the camels grazing pasture. And as they went along they watched the line of the shore. They noted the rocks, the marshy bits and the small inlets.

While the camels grazed, they rested.

Rongus said; "I do not know how good the oil is. I bought the very first I came upon."

"It matters not; good or bad, if it only will burn."

Their plan was set and it was carried out in the following manner. Barzor said; "What are soldiers in Cæsarea are only beggars in Jerusalem." And the meaning of this remark was soon apparent.

Toward evening they took up the halters and led the camels along the sandy shore of the sea in the direction of the city. When they were fairly close they found a small bushy hollow about thirty paces from the edge of the water and here they made their camels kneel.

When it was dark, quite dark, they removed their silken robes and taking out the bags of silver, one by one, and the small bags of gold, they concealed them in the sand, marking the spot with a small uprooted bush. They dragged a long trunk of a fallen palm to the beach and placed it so that one end almost touched the edge of the water while the other end pointed to the bushy place where the camels were tied.

When all was hidden away, they walked down along the shore until they came to the walls of the rich merchant's palace, a distance of almost half a league. Here the sandy beach was very narrow for the high walls were mounted upon jaggy rocks that came close to the shore. Here also they noticed that the water was rough and noisy due to the many rocks in the cove. All this they carefully noted and soon they returned to the place where the camels were secured.

It was now midnight and after resting awhile they started out on another trip along the coast in the opposite direction. Rounding a long point they came to a bay where fishing boats and merchant galleys were moored. As most of the ships were tied to long ropes attached to stakes driven into the sandy shore, they had to walk with great caution. Because of the darkness of the night they could hear the ropes lapping in the water long before they actually came upon them.

Having seen all that was necessary to see in this direction they again returned to the bushy place where their camels were tied. Fearing that someone might come upon these animals by chance, they did not at any time during the night leave the spot for very long.

Content with the condition of the coast and satisfied with the position they had selected, they sat down with their backs against the ribs of one

112

of the camels and refreshed themselves with food and drink. The woolly beasts scenting the food raised their nostrils high and began chewing their everlasting cuds. In this way an hour or two was spent. And now but a short while remained before the streak of dawn would line the sandy edge of the desert far away.

Soon they removed all their clothes and Rongus unbuckled his precious armor. They girdled themselves each with a jackal skin and put knives in their belts. In Barzor's belt was also secured a small tinderbox wrapped tightly in a bit of waxed parchment. Then taking the large jar of oil and a small purse of coins they set out along the coast toward the place where the ships were moored.

Here they selected a small fishing ship, crude and clumsy in its form but rigged with a large square sail. They tied the purse of coins to the mooring rope close to the stake in the sand and waded out into the water holding the large jar between them. Soon they were up to their waists and in another minute the water came even with their ribs. The boat was still some paces ahead.

Rongus placed the jar on his shoulder and he

waited while Barzor swam to the side of the ship. Here he took hold and plumbed the depth. It was over his head. Now he climbed up on the boat and grasping the mooring rope pulled with all his might. Slowly the craft moved forward. At the same time Rongus, with one arm on the jar and the other steadying himself along the rope, came forward until the level of the water was up to his neck. Then Barzor reached over and lifted the jar to the deck of the ship and Rongus climbed up.

As soon as his feet touched the deck of the boat Rongus cut the mooring rope and taking a long pole in hand warped the vessel into deep water. Barzor, in the meantime, busied himself among the ropes of the sail and untied the handle of the rudder.

When the bow pointed to the open sea, Rongus climbed the short mast and loosened the sheets that held the sail. The rough patched cloth dropped and fluttered in the breeze. They made fast the ends and took hold of the tiller. The hull was empty and the boat rode high on the surface. The bow pounded and broke the short stubby waves on top and a salty spray came over from both sides at once.

They sailed out until they were certain they would clear the point; then they rounded gradually and turned down the coast. They looked sharply to see if they could recognize the spot where the camels were resting but the night was still dark and the coast some distance away. Far off ahead of them they could see the black mass of granite that formed the walls and towers of Ben Rashid's palace. And as they sailed about in the open sea they kept this landmark ever in view. But with the first glint of dawn they boldly swung over the rudder and made straight for the rocks.

Now they pierced the sheep-skin that sealed the top of the jar and spilled the oil over the ropes and over the dry portions of the deck. Then Rongus climbed the mast and what remained of the oil he poured over the old sail.

The tiny glint of light in the east, fine as a white thread, soon broadened and the rocks on the coast before the castle were plain before them. Now they were sailing full with the wind and straight into the craggy shore. They headed for a spot between the place where the camels were concealed and the towers of the castle.

In another minute the bottom of the boat scraped a rock hidden under the surface of the water, but the force of the ship's motion sent it on and over.

"Watch out!" cried Barzor.

And as soon as he had said this, the ship struck a second and then a third.

Barzor made ready his flint and steel. There was still another scrape on the bottom before the final crash. They were now within a few steps of the shore and the boat wedged between the rocks began booming and pounding loose its old timbers.

Now the sparks began to fly from Barzor's flint, and in a moment the oil soaked ropes in the stern of the ship broke into a blaze.

"Ready!" Barzor cried. At this signal they jumped into the shallow water and quickly made for the shore.

They ran. It was quite a distance to the place where the bags of silver were hidden in the loose sand and they were blowing hard when they got there. One hasty glance in the hollow to make certain that the camels were still there, then up came the bags of silver and one small bag of gold.

Barzor cut the cords that tied the tops and loaded down under the weight they staggered to the edge of the water. Now they started back in the direction of the blazing ship and as they walked they spilled the coins from the bags upon the sand in a long uneven track. As they went on their loads became lighter and when they came near to the burning wreck pounding on the rocks they gave out loud shouts and terrible cries.

"Help! Help!"

Then they screamed with a terrible cry that seemed to rend the night in shreds.

"Help! Save us! Help."

And again they screamed both together. And they began shouting to each other, crying out anything at all that came to their minds and giving the impression that there were many voices.

"Help! Save us!"

And all the time they shouted, they threw handfuls of silver along the beach and every now and then a few coins of gold.

The ship was now burning with a full blaze.

117

The sail had caught and the flames leaped high. In the half-light of dawn they could see figures moving hurriedly along the walls of the castle.

And once more they cried out and once more they screamed. As soon as they were opposite the burning ship they planted what was left of their silver, making sure that in one place and another quite a handful was heaped together. Then they threw the empty bags away and still crying out "Help! To the rescue! Save us!" they left the shore and waited to see what would happen.

They did not have to wait very long before they saw the gates of the palace open and men with flares come down to the shore. Then they went back slowly, keeping some distance from the water, to the place where the camels were resting.

Here they found everything in order. Rongus strapped on his golden breast-plate and they dressed themselves again in their costly robes. Then untying the legs of the camels they mounted and were off along the fields, keeping clear of the shore.

As soon as they were out of the hollow they could see what remained of the burning boat. Men were running here and there. The light of day was coming on fast. They drove back over the fields slowly and stopped in the shadows of large trees to observe what was going on.

The silver was discovered! There were calls and shouts. And those in the towers and on the walls came running. Soon more and more came pouring out of the castle and some ran back for baskets and other vessels in which to take up the coin. They shouted angry oaths to each other and superiors tried to drive away their subordinates. Still others came and discovered that the coins led in a track down the coast and here they all rushed feeling certain that the main bulk of the treasure had been carried away and the broken coffers had left their trail. Some of the men quarrelled and some were driven back and took to digging in the sand in the places where the coins seemed half buried, and in places where they felt certain something might be found.

Now all seemed quiet about the castle walls.

"Come," said Barzor, "If we cannot take the women now, then they never could be taken?"

IX

•••

Zozo, the black eunuch, was waiting at the garden door.

As soon as he saw the camels approach he cried; "What have I got by standing here? A treasure ship was wrecked on the coast and gold and silver and everybody and . . . What good comes to me by standing here idle?"

The girls were dressed in their finest. Their heads and faces were heavily veiled and their slim ankles and wrists were covered with golden rings. Each carried a bundle of precious belongings and they skipped out lightly across the stone step of the garden door. The two youngest were lifted into the litter behind Rongus while the eldest sister secured herself behind Barzor. Zozo too climbed up and settled himself in this litter, woman fashion. They started off at full speed.

"Now what did I tell you," said the eldest to the black Zozo. "This jolting about is certain to unnerve me. And when I am so unnerved . . . These are nice curtains," she said suddenly, testing the texture with her fingers. "But they should have been longer."

They rode on with all speed. Zozo put his head through the front curtain and said; "You will not forget me, master."

"The hundred pieces are here for you," Barzor replied.

In the other litter one of the girls called out to Rongus; "Say young fellow, we want to stop."

But he paid no attention to her request.

"Say!" She poked him in the back. "Can't you hear me? I say, we want to stop."

"No," said the other with a yawn. "Let him drive on."

"But I want to stop. I want to stop. I want to! I must! Stop!"

Rongus brought the beast to a halt and Barzor seeing this swung his camel around and came beside them.

She put her head out and repeated; "I want to stop."

And the other beside her said; "My sister wants to compose a little verse. She has been inspired."

"And I want to have it written out and sent back to Ben Rashid. We should! We should send him a little verse."

"Oh!" cried Zozo. "They will drive you crazy! Don't listen to them."

"Zozo darling! You must not talk like that." She lifted her veil and stared at him with her full eyes. "I want to stop and I must compose a verse for the flip-flap."

"But sister dear," said the other beside her, "you could compose it in your head and when it was all composed we could stop. Why stop now?"

"Yes," added Barzor kindly. "When it is all perfected in your head we will stop at the first town and order a scribe to take it down on clean parchment. Then we will send it back by messenger."

She seemed pleased. She laughed and clapped her

hands and shook the rings on her wrists gaily. "We will. We will. That's what we will do."

And now everyone seemed satisfied, and off they started again at full speed.

But under his breath Barzor said; "What a pretty crew of feather-pated gibble-gabblers!"

Soon the two girls discovered that there were nuts and dried-fruit and sweet things in the camel bags and they made Rongus drive faster so they could overtake their sister in the other litter and learn what she found, and make certain that she had nothing different. Then the one who wanted to compose, declaimed a few lines with her mouth full of food, something quite profane, and failing to make a single rhyme she soon gave it up and amused herself by toying with the rings on her ankles.

The other one who was with her kept folding and unfolding a bit of cloth while she sang in Greek a little child's ditty. Between the verses she stopped long enough to eat some nuts.

In the other litter the eldest said to Zozo; "You are sure they will take us to the governor and he will send us home?"

"Yes. It is all arranged. They are princes of the blood and they have given their word. It is all in the name of justice."

"Well anyway," she replied, "I always wanted to see Jerusalem."

Zozo said; "Who is to say how much I lost by waiting at the garden door? . . . Why they had to select a night when gold and silver was free on the beach, I can't understand! Everybody will come back rich while I had to be waiting at the garden door. . . . I had bad luck in my childhood and it has ever been with me."

"Wait until Ben Rashid lays hands on you," said the eldest sister. "Then you will cry in a different tune. He will give you the luck you deserve. He will break every bone in your juiceless body."

"He will never see me again."

"He will rake the four ends of the earth until he finds you. And when he finds you . . ."

"Well what of it? Supposing I go and tell him that you ran away and I couldn't hold you back."

"He will cut strips of flesh from your black body, and every piece that he cuts he will throw to

124

the dogs. And you will see with your own eyes how they eat your muscle and your blood."

"Then I won't go back to him."

"And who will look after his other women?"

"Let him hire Roman gladiators, for all I care."

"Gladiators in the harem!"

"Who then is strong enough to hold you women?"

"What pleasant thoughts. Really, Zozo, you are a darling."

"First you torture me, then you . . ."

"No, I do not."

"Yes, you say he will break my bones and cut pieces from me to feed dogs. And you say all things to frighten me. . . . And everybody else will be rich from the treasure on the beach and here I am. . . . And what have I got." He was near tears.

"Poor Zozo, poor Zozo."

"And the other women wanted me to take them also. They were ready to pay me well. But what have I got from you?"

"If you bring us home, Zozo, you will be rewarded with presents fit for a king."

"Another harem!"

"No, Zozo. With gold and silver and fine silks and glass bottles filled with fragrant oils for your hair, and perhaps a slave of your own and maybe a whole house with a wall about it and a garden of flowers."

"I think I could do better with the Governor of Judea."

"How?"

"Well he has soldiers and secretaries and there are ambassadors from distant lands that arrive after long journeys and there would be great feasts and good wine."

"Tut, tut, but not for you."

"Yes, for me too, if I only held the keys."

"What keys?"

"The same that I held for Ben Rashid."

"And you think he would trust you with the women's quarters."

He shrugged his shoulders. "I know how to please them."

"For a penny you would sell us all."

"I sell only those who want to be sold."

"Some day you will be beaten until your skin

126

is white and for three months you will not be able
to stir."

"There you go again."

"And you will not only be beaten but your
limbs will be twisted out of their sockets and . . ."

"Don't torture me!" he cried in his whining
voice.

"I don't torture you, I only say what you deserve
and you know it is coming to you."

"And by this time they are all rich from the
scattered treasure and here I am in a cage with a
female tiger."

"Go ride with the others."

"I don't want to."

"They will treat you better."

"No. They won't. They are even worse."

She laughed and arranged her hair with her small
white fingers. After a few minutes she ate some
nuts and said; "Poor Zozo." Then she took a bite
of some fruit and; "Here eat the other half, it is
too bitter for me."

But Zozo was angry and he threw it out upon
the ground. Barzor seated in the opening of the
litter drove on with all possible speed and he heard

every word that was spoken between the eldest sister and the eunuch.

Rongus, however, enjoyed a different kind of conversation. After the two sisters had eaten as much as they pleased they licked the stickiness from their fingers and opening their bundles began to kohl their eyes with the aid of a small silver mirror. But the restless tossing of the running camel made their task almost impossible. Their bracelets clanked.

"Hey, you," cried one. "Can't you drive easier?"

Then the other said; "You churn us up so that we cannot hold the clothes on our backs."

"Really it is true. We are all undone."

Then to each other; "What a handsome driver we have?"

"He looks a dear," added one.

And saying this, one of these papery chits sprawled out and hung her little foot forward beside Rongus. Then she shook her ankle and clinked the rings. But as soon as Rongus caught sight of it she quickly drew it away and laughed.

"Say, my pretty one," said the other. "Come sit with us and let the camel go as she pleases."

"There is no room inside," Rongus replied.

"We would make room."

"They may soon be on our tracks and there is no time to be lost."

"Say, smart, aren't you? Suppose you do lose time, don't we lose something too?"

Rongus was silent and one of the girls ran her fingers along the back of his neck. They giggled.

"Stop," he cried.

They laughed.

"So handsome and we must stop. Tut, tut. Dear me!"

And the other said: "My, my: I could cry. My, my: I will die."

And they laughed again.

Suddenly one of them discovered a small rent in the cloak that Rongus wore. She put in her picking finger to explore and drew it back quickly. Then she signaled her sister and they peeped into the opening.

"A golden armor," whispered one.

The other nodded and then spoke aloud; "Oh, noble and magnificent prince, where are you taking us?"

"To Jerusalem."

"And then where?"

"To the governor himself."

"And what would Pontius Pilate want with us?"

"Yes," added the other. "What is a Greek to a Roman?"

"But answer me, my noble and magnificent prince. Tell us, darling, what would Pontius Pilate do with us?"

"How should I know?"

They laughed.

"Then I propose we all go home with you."

Rongus shook his head. He kept his thoughts to himself. 'Yesterday, or so it seemed, I was a quarry slave. It seems only yesterday when I saw the girl of my dream. Yesterday, there was Sulla with his lash, and yesterday the golden crown came out of Herod's tomb with the jar of Cleopatra's spices and yesterday—or was it the day before?—I stood before my uncle and everything seems only yesterday. For seven years I have toiled for the Romans, with one day like another, and now all within a single week everything has happened.' These were the thoughts that ran through his mind.

"Take us all home with you," pleaded the other.

And again he shook his head but never spoke a word.

"And who is the governor?" said one mockingly.

"Another flip-flap," answered her sister laughing.

"A Roman filled with *posca!*" The legions in warm countries demanded a thirst-quencher, and this was the name of the cheap diluted wine-vinegar that was part of the soldiers' rations.

"Cheap beer and *posca!*"

"Now listen," commanded one. "You take us home and don't care what anyone says."

"And we will please you; we know how. Don't we, sister?"

"If the three of us are unable to please, then nobody will be able to accomplish it."

"What do you say?"

Rongus shook his head.

"But we would rather be with you than with the fat old Roman squeeze."

131

For seven years Rongus had been sweated by the Romans and all this free and loose talk pleased him immensely. Nevertheless he kept his mouth closed.

"Oh, well," said one of the girls reclining her papery figure against the large cushion tied to the camel's hump, "there are others."

"And some won't need asking."

"Dear me," yawned the first, "I am so bored." She played with the golden rings on her wrists and they tinkled with the up and down of the camel.

In this way they rode on until the sun was high over their heads and at last they arrived at a fairly large town.

"You will buy us something, won't you, darling?"

Rongus asked what they needed.

"Two more rings. Two more for each of us."

But the other said; "No. Buy us pins. It's really necessary. We can hardly hold the clothes on our backs so violently do you shake us."

Then the sisters quarrelled. One cried; "Rings," and the other cried; "Pins."

Then Barzor drawing up beside this commotion asked what was going on. When Rongus told him, Barzor drew a deep breath and said; "The two you have are no different from the sample in my litter. They are chittish fractions, all of one piece!"

But the quarrel did not subside. "Rings!" insisted the first. "Pins!" sulked the other.

Soon they came into the narrow streets of the town. Barzor and Rongus dismounted and led their camels to the market place. Here Barzor bought three rolls of large silver pins, tied in bright colored wools each containing ten in number. To pacify the girls Rongus handed them up without delay. They quickly untied the rolls and began counting them over and over to make certain that each had received alike. They used their fingers in counting.

While they were thus occupied, Barzor found a scribe sitting before his booth.

"Have you fine parchment?"

"The best in Judea."

"Is it flat and evenly cut?"

"It is even doubly split and polished with bone."

"Then let me see it."

"Large or small?"

"Large."

133

He produced a roll.

"But this is yellow."

"I have white also, but it is more costly."

"Bring it out."

He untied a bundle from which he selected the largest and best. Barzor seemed content and asked; "What are your letters like?"

"Here are writings in Latin, Greek and Aramaic. I also know the holy script." By that he meant Hebrew.

"I want you to write in Latin and make your letters with grace. Write as I dictate."

"To prevent mistake, first I will do it on the wax slate and then I will copy it in sepia."

The scribe took his metal stylus in hand.

"To his excellency, Pontius Pilate, Governor. . . ."

The scribe looked up in amazement.

"Write as I dictate: To his excellency, Pontius Pilate, Governor of Judea, magnificent in manner and merciful in judgment. Grateful of the many favors extended to me and of the free and safe passage granted the gifts for the Holy Temple, I send you with my loyal messengers the three prize

Greek girls and may their loveliness melt misfortune and drive away anxiety."

Zozo came down from the litter to see what was going on.

"We could do with a little fragrant hair-oil," he said, interrupting the writing of the document.

"Presently you shall have it. But now while you are here, decide for yourself. Do you want to be free or will you go with the girls into the palace?"

"What does one do when one is free?"

"One may do as one chooses. But if you would live decently you must work."

"You mean with my legs or with my arms?"

"At some trade, or with a merchant, or in the fields."

"No, I should not like that at all. I would rather stay with the Greek girls."

Turning to the scribe, Barzor asked; "What were your last words?"

He read; "Melt misfortune and drive away anxiety."

"Good. Then add as follows: And their faithful slave-eunuch accompanies them. May you be pleased to accept this humble gift from your most devoted subject."

The scribe repeated the words slowly as he wrote them on the wax-coated tablet.

"Now," said Barzor. "Sign it: Ben Rashid of Alexandria."

"Good," added Zozo, who also felt he was part of this important document. "I would have much better chances in the palace. There will be soldiers and secretaries . . . and ambassadors will come from distant lands and they will all need refreshing. And why should the rivers of pleasure run to waste? In fact, I would even pay out my own money not to be encumbered with freedom. For what is the life of a free man? Toil and strife. And what is his lot? Poverty and wretchedness. And what . . ."

"Stop! You are talking nonsense."

"Forgive me, master. But you won't forget the rest of the money due me?"

"You shall have it at once."

He paid him what had been promised and while the beautiful parchment roll was being written Barzor wandered along the row of perfumers' booths and bought the fragrant hair-oil. Zozo lost no time in bringing the vial to his mistress.

Now the girl, who only a very short time before had insisted on composing a verse for their former master and had brought the entire company to a halt with her obstinacy—now as they stood before the booth of the scribe she could easily have fulfilled her desire. But, alas! She had failed to make anything rhyme and the whole matter had by this time left her foolish head completely.

In the meantime Rongus had watered the camels, inspected the soft pads of their feet, tightened the belly cords and held everything in readiness for departure. And in a few minutes, the parchment roll was fully executed, the scribe paid and, refreshed by the pause, they were off again at full speed.

Avoiding the main roads as much as possible, they cut across the low, black gravel hills and while these pebbly paths offered poor footing for the laden camels, time was nevertheless saved.

The eldest sister sampled the oil on the palms of her fragile white hands. Closing the front curtain she undid her hair and, unpinning her dress, let it

137

fall to her waist so that it would not be soiled by the heavy oil. Zozo took the comb from her bundle and began his task by first combing out the tangled ends. Her pure white skin glowed in the semi-darkness of the litter and Zozo's jet bulky figure hovered over her with his pink palms gently stroking her black flowing hair. She closed her eyes as the camels ran on and on.

Cutting across the top of a desolate hill they came to a rocky place where the path wound about a limestone ledge. Suddenly before them they saw a mop of bright woolen cords mounted upon a pole. They approached with caution. The red wool dyed with a mountain berry had been bleached to a violet pink by many suns. And before them they saw the outcast leper who had placed this warning signal before his wretched shelter. His home was less than a tomb; it was merely a hole in the limestone ledge and so low that he could only creep in or out. Before it was a mat woven of straw and on this mat stood a clay pot for water and beside it a crust that seemed green with mold.

The unfortunate man pulled himself out of the hole and reclined on the straw. His eyes bulged in their sockets; there was yellow about his cheeks and his skinny, bloodless limbs resembled unbaked dough sprinkled with white flour.

"Mercy for an outcast!"

Barzor stopped to throw him a coin and as he did so the Greek girl, half naked in the litter, lifted an edge of the curtain.

"Hold a moment, Zozo," she said, and she removed a golden bracelet from her ankle and threw it out upon the ground.

"Mercy for an outcast! Bless you! Bless you! May the heavens shower their abundance upon you. Bless you! Bless you! Pause a moment, and I will cast before you the past and the future. I was honest, I was faithful, I was pious, I sang the praises of the Lord, I loved my wife, I acted in kindness, and I paid with loyalty, friendship, and devotion. The past is far behind and the present is . . . here you see me before you; this is what man comes to. And the wolf and the fox, they too have their holes in the ground. And they too are outcasts. And the warm blood of my flesh becomes white to mark the great turning in the world. And I cast before you a prophecy born in misery and delivered in the deep of night and when I creep into this dark hole the whole world lights up before me and I see the color of what is to be. Man will thrive by cunning, he will advance by trickery, the dishonest will ride in the saddles of kings and the faithless will be the princes of the world. And the pious will be sunk and enfeebled while the blasphemous will rise up and prosper with all abundance. And man will live with woman in jiggery and he will laugh a bawdy laugh. And for kindness he will give grossness, loyalty will turn to fraud, and devotion will twist into revenge. Man embroiled with his fellow man will become a brutal fighter and the whole world will be his battle field. The soft and tender will perish, and the crusty and those without pity, the depraved, the ruthless, the lawless, tricksters, scamps, spies and rogues—all these will be the grand inheritors. And they will smile with the sly smirk of the serpent, for to them all will belong."

While the first camel paused, the second drew up with Rongus and the two girls, who seeing their sister's bracelet on the ground at once removed each an ankle ring and threw it before the declaiming outcast. In the ways of compassion they had been well brought up.

"And now I have given you my vision. The past you know. The miserable present creeps before you and the future—may we never live to see the day —is not for the tender and not for the merciful. May the heavens protect you in your journey and defend you in your need. Bless you! Bless you!"

They drove on through the rocks and down the slope of the hill. Once firm upon level ground they started up a rolling jog that brought them on with great speed.

"Well there goes a good bracelet for nothing," said one.

The other leaned forward and asked of Rongus; "What will he do with the bracelets?"

"Camel drivers and peddlers with mules come across the hills and will bring him what he wants. But often they take the poor man's coins and never return or if they do they are certain to cheat him."

"Poor man," said one. "We should have given him another bracelet."

"What, two from each? Then he would have six. No, I don't think I could spare another one."

141

"Well, we get them back, don't we?"

"How will we get them back?"

"Why, of course, the fat Do-do must return to us what we have expended. Of course. You do not think. . . . Well, my dear sister, you are truly simple. The fat Do-do . . ."

"Who?"

"Why, Pilate, of course. Are we not travelling to him and at his request? And should he not provide all that is necessary for the journey? And are we not ladies of rank? And being ladies of rank we must give with generosity, for such is our position and certainly it is expected of us. But the old Do-do must pay us back. Really it is all for him, for it surely is no pleasure for us to throw away our bracelets. That he must of course understand."

The empty-headed creatures, exquisite in face and ivory in figure, chatted on and on. Their words with little meaning were accompanied by the tinkling clink of their rings set into vibration by the roll of the running camel.

And so, with this kind of music, Barzor and Rongus pushed forward and soon arrived in Jerusalem.

142

X

AND now they led the littered camels along the narrow streets of the city winding their way through the jostling crowds until they came to the stone arch connecting the rear wall of the Temple with one of the turrets of Antonia. This palace of towers was the home of the Governor of Judea, and his Roman soldiers could pass freely from the towers, over the arch and along the rear wall of the Temple and from here down a broad flight of steps into their long barracks beneath the level of the streets.

In the street beside the arch there was a short flight of steps that led to the main entrance of the

143

towers. And between these steps and the side of the arch was Pilate's seat of judgment, covered with a bright awning held in position by several long spears. As the pious Jews were forbidden by tradition from entering the home of a heathen, or even so much as crossing the threshold of an unblessed hovel, Pontius Pilate had to come into the public street to hold court and try the offenders who were daily brought before him. The priests of the Temple, however, came into the Towers whenever necessary.

Barzor and Rongus arrived with the fair Greek girls just when the court was breaking up. The prisoners were led off, the soldiers tramped down the street and the governor with his Greek and Hebrew secretaries, together with the scribes, recorders and military chiefs, left the protection of the canopy and came leisurely up the steps and into the guarded entrance of the Towers. The picked Roman guards stood at attention with spears erect and chins high, their brass helmets and trappings brightly polished, as the jolly company, content with all the judgments of the day, passed into the fortress.

The officers and secretaries spoke their opinions freely in the hearing of the governor.

"Have you news from Sulla?" asked one.

"He is in the dungeon," answered one of the officers.

They laughed.

"Well, it was coming to him," said a scribe.

"That and more."

"I wager he sold the chariot and horses."

"Not at the cost of his teeth," answered another.

Again they laughed.

"I wish I knew the truth of it all."

"Well, I certainly cannot believe his story."

"Perhaps when he cools off in the dungeon, then he will confess and say what he really did with the chariot."

"How much longer must he remain in confinement?"

"I don't know. But I suppose he will be let out in about a week unless. . . ."

"Unless what?"

"Unless his excellency orders his release sooner."

"No, no!" protested Pilate laughing. "I do not interfere in such cases. We have enough with the

Goshen College Library

natives and mad prophets and wild mountain
preachers, to say nothing of the fanatical priests
right here that need all our attention. He has his
officers and they know Roman law. A man loses
his chariot, his breast-plate and arms; and he loses
also his horses and his own teeth. I suppose he will
want me to pay him for his losses."

Again they laughed.

"Yes. Give him back his teeth!" cried one.

And in this way, laughing and joking, they came
into the big hall, a narrow though long colonnade,
and here, at one end, the tables were spread with
refreshments.

The moment they were heard approaching,
Buncha, a female Babylonian dwarf, cried out to
warn the servants; "Here they come! Hello!
Hello!" And saying this she skipped about on her
short stubby legs and ran along the line of columns,
with a weaving motion, in front of one and behind
the next. "Ho! Ho! Hello, hello!"

This strange little woman, no higher than the
waist of an ordinary person, deformed in hip and
spine, had long arms that almost reached the
ground. She was a hideous, misshapen human bun-

146

dle, grim at one moment and a clown the next. She
was over thirty years old, but she was spry as an
ape. She was wise as the seven sages, yet her fooling
tongue and tricks were known even as far as Rome.
She was the unholy terror of the Towers, and the
chief source of joy. But this active human stump
was also the power behind the throne.

She came from Babylon a slave, yet nobody in
the whole of Judea enjoyed so much freedom. She
would pull the reeds out of the scribes' hands and
destroy the rolls of the secretaries; she would unbuckle the swords of the highest officers as they
stood in dignity before the court and, if they protested, she would return slyly to unbuckle more.
Even Pilate himself, rendering serious judgment,
she did not hesitate to interrupt. In one room and
out of the next she skipped, her legs too short to
walk. And when she would interrupt Pilate,
whether because she did not like his verdict, or for
some other reason, she would call him an ass, or a
pig or a ninny-fool and with a final retort she
would pipe out; "And if you don't like it, come
and catch me." With these words off she would
skip. And often when she was out of hearing,

Pilate seeing the blunt reason of her remarks, would reverse his judgment.

A large wooden key with metal teeth was always at Buncha's belt, and the door that it unlocked led to the women's private quarters. But besides opening and locking the door she also used the key in other ways. No soldier held a readier weapon.

"Hello! Hello!" she cried, seeing them enter the room. She skipped about between the columns. "It's duck, today. Roasted brown with green sauce, and stuffed with livers and olives. Hello! Hello! And barley broth. And rings of dough boiled before baking. And sweet tarts stuffed with poppy-seed ground in honey. And watermelons and berries. Hello! And two wines; cinnamon and lotus, bitter and sweet. One cup for the thirsty, two for the weary, and three for the witless. Hello! Hello!"

"Buncha, Buncha!" they called. "Come here, Buncha."

She stood still. "Why should I go there, when you must and will come here." She pointed to the table.

Without ceremony they began eating; some

148

were seated and some were standing and she walked among them.

"Here, what is that you are munching, let me see. Oh, a leg." She took it out of the secretary's hand and tasting it critically added; "Well, pretty good," and handed it back. "Nothing but the best for you, even if I must sample every morsel."

"Here Buncha, eat a cake."

She broke off a crumb. "Lard!" she said. "Phu! The food of the devil. Here, give me more."

And they all laughed.

"I tell you," she continued. "Soon I shall grow horns. Great big twisty ones." And turning to Pilate; "And how would his excellency like me in horns?"

"I would have golden thimbles made to protect the points."

"From friends or enemies?"

"My dear Buncha, when you grow horns, you may use them as you please; friends or enemies."

"Good. I will start on the friends, for then there will be fewer enemies."

"Many?"

"A good many."

Again they laughed and drank some wine from small bowls made of polished amber.

"Here, Buncha," said one of the secretaries. "Eat some of these nuts."

She took a handful and ate. "See," she said, "the ass and I eat out of the same manger."

"Yes, Buncha. You and I should really eat out of one manger."

"The straw would go to your head and the grain to my feet."

Then she noticed that Pilate was drinking wine.

"Watch out," she warned. "It's your third cup."

"But the cups are small."

"Remember what they say: 'One cup—a lamb; two cups—a lion and three cups—a swine.'"

"Ha, ha. You are a female rick and the demons gave you a forked tongue."

"True, your Excellency, true. But the tongue that laps the wine in lets the secret slip out."

"Quite right, Buncha. You speak good sense always. I really think you should have been born a man."

"Then I might have been a scribe or secretary or something equally foolish, or perhaps even a gov-

ernor of a Roman province. As it is I am a fool
and that is exactly how one becomes wise. But no
half-measures; you must be very, very foolish,
otherwise you cannot be wise."

At this moment a page-boy came into the hall
with a parchment roll, the same that was supposed
to have been written by Ben Rashid of Alexandria. Pilate read the document and ordered that
all should be brought before him. Beside the table
were some large seats and long marble benches and
Buncha ran about and saw that all were properly
seated for the occasion.

Barzor and the three Greek girls, covered from
head to foot and tinkling their rings came forward.
Behind them walked Rongus and the black Zozo
with the three cloth bundles belonging to his mis-
tresses.

The girls looked to the right and left and with
their peeping eyes took in as much as possible. They
certainly saw everything there was to see in a few
glances—nothing, from the food on the table to
the thick arms and legs of Pontius Pilate, escaped
their notice.

And one whispered to the other as they came

forward; "The old Do-do is not so fat as I thought."

"He looks quite jolly."

But the eldest was silent.

As they came to a halt before Pilate, Barzor said; "Here I have delivered safely the present from our good master."

"Good!" piped out Buncha with a squeak. "What's good about him?"

And the eldest of the Greek girls lifted her veil and turning to the Babylonian dwarf said; "You are right. Ben is nothing but an old flip-flap."

"Hush!" called Zozo. "You forget where you are."

"I said nothing bad."

"Let her speak as she will," replied Buncha putting her hand to the large key in her belt. And this marked the first encounter between the dwarf and the black eunuch.

"At any rate," continued Barzor, "we have done our duty and we will soon return to our home."

"Your master has many homes."

"We come from Cæsarea, may it please your excellency."

Buncha came forward and inspected the big black negro from head to foot. She looked up at his full height and she noticed the money tied to his belt.

Pilate unrolled the parchment and read its contents aloud to the entire company.

"It reads very nice," said Buncha, and walking around the girls to see them better from all sides she added; "And they smell nice, too. But what do we know?"

"What should we know?" asked Pilate.

"Ah, with women you should know everything, for even then you will know little enough. A bad girl is like a long day of rain. I believe we should see their faces."

Now the eldest sister did lift her veil when she had spoken but she let it fall again, but when this was said the three of them removed their veils and stood proudly before the company. They knew the strength of their beauty.

Buncha laughed. "There, that's good. Now the cat is out of the bag. Ha, ha, very nice indeed." She saw at a glance that the three girls were of a very rare vintage and the horrible twistings of her own monstrous figure taught her what points to admire in feminine beauty.

"And are you girls content to come to Jerusalem?" asked Pilate.

"I always wanted to see Jerusalem," said the eldest.

And the second added; "If you will treat us well we will be happy to remain."

While the third said; "Of course. We are very pleased to come. Ben was good to us but as my sister has already told you he was nothing but an old flip-flap. He was not a father, nor a brother, and neither was he a husband nor a lover. He was just plain nothing."

At this all laughed.

Buncha skipped about and said; "Really, the dolls are alive! They speak! Let me see, do their little hearts beat?" She put her hand to the bosom of the girl nearest her. "Pitter-pat. Pitter-pat. Upon my word, they are alive."

Zozo did not seem to like this for he stepped quickly between the dwarf and his mistress but Buncha pretended not to see him and with her clumsy stumps she stamped on his feet.

All this time Rongus was silent. He looked about and searched the faces of the Roman officers but there was none he knew. He breathed more freely when he had made certain that Sulla was not among them.

"We should like a bill," said Barzor, "to take back to our master saying that we have delivered our charge safely and that all are hale and sound."

Pilate signaled one of the secretaries who immediately began to write out the requested document.

Buncha now ran up and down in great agitation. "Hale and sound! Well, I declare. What do we know? What have we seen? They are probably deformed and camel-humped!"

"We are not," said the girls.

"Or perhaps they are maimed and all bone. And probably they are dry like salt-fish."

"No, we are not!"

"Or who should know; maybe they are flat as a bench, and underneath they are black and. . . ."

"No, no, no!"

"Hairy, and have dugs like a cow."

"No! We are not! We are not!"

They protested violently and stamped their feet

155

and shook the rings on their wrists. This last was an insult that they could not endure and, slipping out their white arms, they let the bodice of their robes fall to their waists. Three pairs of dove-like breasts, all cast from the same twin molds, were open for all to gaze upon.

"There, now are you satisfied?" said the eldest.

But Zozo protested at this public exhibition and began to cover them up when Buncha pulled out her great key with its metal teeth and tapped him smartly across his black fingers.

"She's the devil's tooth!" he cried.

"Stand back you black night of sin!"

She held the key in her hand and forced the big negro back to the rear of the hall.

"Now you stay there," she said.

But Zozo under his breath said; "You female frog!"

It was true she did look something like a frog at that moment. But then she straightened up and skipped about pretending to be very merry.

All this time the girls stood naked to their waists waiting for Buncha to take back her words.

"Well," said one. "Will you admit you were wrong?"

"I will admit it before all. Clear butter would melt in jealousy. And white marble was never cut so fine. These are daughters of lilies indeed, with their morning dew unshaken."

Then she bowed and went up to Barzor. "You see this big key," she said. "I will lock them up and see that they are safe from harm. And I keep the key in my belt. See, here, like this."

But instead of putting it in her belt she began forcing it under Barzor's sash. He laughed at the joke.

"Oh," said Buncha. "What a mistake I have made! I thought your sash was my belt. Ha, ha! How funny!"

Everyone laughed.

When the girls heard the pretty speech of the Babylonian dwarf and how they were compared to white marble and lilies, they were content and placed their arms back into the sleeves of their loose robes.

In the meantime the small square of parchment was made ready. Pilate took the reed in hand and signed his name and, removing the large ring from his finger, he pressed his seal into the wax beside his signature.

"Here," he said. "This diploma of safe-conduct will take you back with full acknowledgment of the gift of your master."

Barzor took it quickly and, after bowing low, departed with haste. Rongus followed closely on his heels and before they were fully out of the long hall they again heard the Babylonian dwarf threaten poor Zozo.

"You black plague!" she cried. "I will begin now to teach you your place."

XI

AFTER Buncha had unlocked the door leading to the private section of the Towers and ordered the matrons to prepare the bath and do everything necessary for the three Greek girls, she gave Zozo a final peck with her key and returned in haste.

"Move the bench over a bit," she ordered one of the officers and with his aid she climbed up so that she could reach Pilate's ear.

"They are as white as snow," she whispered.

Pilate smiled.

"Really they are lovely. Too lovely."

"You might say the honey is too sweet or the gold too pure."

159

"They seem too willing," said the dwarf.

"And you might say the warriors are too strong and the horses too swift."

"They do not tell everything."

"How do you know?"

"When beauty is eager to display itself then you may be certain there is something she is holding back."

"What they conceal we shall soon see," Pilate replied.

"And the black plague of a eunuch is more than a plain attendant."

"Why?"

"He has too much money in his belt."

"It might be food or nuts that he is carrying."

"No, it is coin. I felt it."

"We will watch him."

"And the young Jew who was silent is not a camel driver."

"How could you tell that?"

"Because there was a small rent in his cloak and he wore a metal breast-plate beneath."

"And did the other have the same?"

160

"No. He carried a large dagger underneath, but no armor."

"Are you sure?"

"Yes. I pretended to put the key into his sash and I felt with my hands."

"But that is nothing. It is natural for a person conducting a precious gift across the desert to have with him the means of protection."

"Yes, true enough," she whispered. "But he does not live in Cæsarea."

"How can you know such a thing?

"I know. I am certain. I smelled his garments and there was no trace of the sea in them. The salt that adheres to the cloth was not there and the garments were not new."

"What is it then?"

"And the young Jew with the breast-plate underneath was not a servant, nor was he a warrior in the employ of Ben Rashid. Because his hands were too rough and the hardness of the palms could come only through violent labor and the cracks in the skin only from lime, or the dust of limestone."

"But what can it all mean?"

"And if the young Jew were a servant of Ben

Rashid, who is also a Jew, why should he be dressed in Arab cloth?"

"Then why?"

"More I can not say. The young Jew does not belong to Ben Rashid but he belongs to the old Arab. He walked behind him."

"Perhaps they were hired by Ben Rashid to conduct the girls safely?"

"No! That I can not believe, for Ben Rashid has more caravans coming and going than any merchant in Judea; and the larger the caravan the safer the merchandise."

"What then!"

"These are two who have sprung from the bowels of the earth, and they come with a purpose."

"But now they are gone. If you had only told me all this sooner then we might have. . ."

"Reason cannot jump like a mad dog. It walks slowly to see what lies concealed behind the curtains."

"And of all these facts you are certain?"

"Most certain," answered Buncha.

"But what lies behind?" Pilate moved uneasily.

"Here are the girls and what could be the plot? We must question them."

"They will tell little, for they understand even less. And you must remember they are white as snow. But the black slave must know all."

"Watch carefully, Buncha. Until we know more of all this, see that there is no contact between these girls and the other women."

"True. It will be hard to hold them, but I will watch."

"And the Arab and the young Jew, what will they now do?"

"Ah, that is not so easy to guess. But there is grit in their manner and they are filled with a determination that could sweep the very sand out of the desert."

Pilate jumped from his seat and cried; "Bring them back! The Arab and the young Jew! Give chase and bring them before me!"

The officers ran through the hall and down the steps. But Barzor and Rongus were already out of sight.

The guards at the gate pointed in the direction they had taken. The officers ran back into the

163

towers; then they suddenly appeared running along the path over the arch, across the wall of the Temple and soon their gorgeously plumed brass helmets disappeared beneath the wall as they descended into the barracks.

The chains clanked as the iron gates of the barracks were unlocked and four chariots started off. Two runners on foot went ahead cutting a path through the swarms of people in the streets and crying out; "Make room! Give way! In the name of Cæsar! At your peril! Make way!"

The crowds divided in the middle and, falling back, pressed into the stalls that lined the streets. Some of the baskets and loose boards displaying provisions and wares were upset by this sudden surge and the merchants cursed. The chariots rumbled over the rough cobbles and the metal shoes on the horses' hoofs scraped the surface and threw out sparks.

The outrunners went only as far as the south gate of the city and here, panting for breath, they inquired of the watchmen what road had been taken by two littered camels and their drivers.

"The one straight in the middle. Toward Bethlehem!"

The driver of the first chariot heard the direction. He whipped up his horses and the other followed. Outside the gate the road was fairly clear of crowds and stray travellers kept well to one side.

The drivers let loose the reins and cracked their whips. The wheels of the chariots bumped over the tops of the rough cobbles as the pace increased. They rushed on. Soon they were going full speed and the heavy pounding of the horses' hoofs was heard far ahead of them and those seeing them approach as a noisy cloud of dust stood aside and gave them plenty of room.

But the journey to Bethlehem was in distance only two leagues and Barzor and Rongus had lost no time in getting under way. They had already covered more than half the distance when glancing back from an elevated spot they saw the four chariots start out along the road.

Now they pressed on and coming to a small path that led off to the left they suddenly turned. At the same time they untied the curtains of the litters and rolled them up in a compact bundle which

165

they tucked under the large pillow. Then they cut the cords that held the sticks and framework together and one by one these dropped into the desert sand until nothing of the high square form remained and the camels were running bare. Thus stripped of all superficial trappings they should have been able to get up greater speed but a bad stretch of rough soft sand delayed them. Once this was passed they turned the heads of the camels in the direction of the main road. They removed their turbans and waited in a small ravine concealed from the road.

They did not wait very long before they heard the chariots approach and pass with a rushing clatter and a pounding stamp of the horses' hoofs. When these swift racers were well down the road they came up from the hollow and proceeded upon their journey in a most leisurely and unconcerned fashion.

And Barzor said to Rongus, pointing to the small square of parchment rolled up and safe in the breast of his cloak; "It was a lot of trouble and all for a bit of official writing. But this is the document we need and now we can play in earnest."

166

"If all this was only half in earnest then what you would call really earnest must tumble down the very walls of cities."

"Cities indeed!"

Back in Bethlehem, Yaba, the gray-headed Arab, who only a short time before sat so long and patiently before his basket of merchandise and his small box of amber in the market place awaiting the arrival of Barzor to direct him to the little walled house that he had hired, now once more awaited his chief. He sat in the fields north of the city gate. The asses grazed nearby among some stubby tree-laurel. Small birds mainly larks and finches hopped about from bush to bush and every now and then a bulbul would pipe out its clear sharp note.

But beyond all this peace and quiet suddenly Yaba saw the cloud of dust raised by the onrushing chariots. He came near to the edge of the road to see them better as they passed.

The first chariot driver threw his weight on the reins and called out. "Two littered camels! In the name of Cæsar! An Arab and a young Jew. Did you see them pass?"

"Only a moment ago! They were dressed in silks!"

" 'Tis they! Which way?"

"Ahead and around the city to the right. Then on the road to Herodium. But you must hasten to catch them."

"Catch them!" he cried. "They must have wings!"

"Wings indeed, for the feet of their camels barely touched the ground!"

"This way!" called the leader and off they went in the direction indicated by the cunning Yaba.

But Yaba knew from this incident that his master could not be very far away and waited.

Back in Jerusalem a different kind of search had begun in the Towers. Pilate and the frog-shaped Babylonian dwarf went into the women's quarters. They found Zozo sitting alone.

"They are still in the bath," he explained. "They do not want to come out at all and I am wearied waiting for them."

"What are they doing there so long?" Pilate inquired.

168

"Nothing. Splashing water and trying to catch the little fish with their hands."

"They will come soon; they are only playing," said Buncha.

"I tell them what they should do but they do not listen to me. They torture me all day long."

The simple minded negro thought that this complaint would gain the sympathy and favor of the governor.

But Buncha removed the big key from her belt and, holding it aloft, threatened Zozo until he cried out; "It's the truth I tell you. They spend their whole time thinking up new ways to torture me. I was unfortunate in my youth and ever since bad fortune has tracked after me."

"Misfortune grips one around the neck and not in the belt," added Buncha pointing to the bag of money.

Zozo was confused.

"Silver or gold?" demanded the female dwarf.

"It is not mine. Really it is not. It belongs to the girls and they trust me with it as they would trust me with anything—even their virtue."

169

"Gold and virtue are oil and water—they cannot be mixed."

"I tell you the money is theirs."

"And how much did you get for bringing the girls here?"

"Nothing. It's not true. We are sent here by Ben Rashid himself."

"You black bones of sin! Soot of evil! Corrupter of honesty and stain of fraud! What has Ben Rashid to do with it all?"

"He . . . He . . ." his voice weakened. "He sent us here."

"Then we will keep the girls and send you back."

"No. No. He would not like it. He would beat me because I did not please you. He would cut pieces from my flesh and throw them to dogs. And the girls might die without me. Really, they would die."

"Why would they die?"

"Because they are devoted, they love me so. And they would pine away without me."

The dwarf winked to Pilate and he could not keep from laughing.

170

"Now tell the truth. How much did the Arab give you?" continued the merciless dwarf.

"He gave me all you see."

"There. Now it will be easier. And why?"

"Because he is a prince and he took a liking to me."

"And where is Ben Rashid now?"

"He will be home today or tomorrow."

"In which home?"

"In Cæsarea."

"Good. And what will be the first thing that he will do?"

"How should I know?"

"Oh yes. You know. What will be his first cry?"

"Really I don't know. You cannot expect me to know what an oracle himself would not know."

"But you do know! Will he not cry out: 'The girls have been stolen!' What then?"

"Yes. If he does not say so himself, they will cry it out for him. . . . But you won't send me back, will you? It would be terrible!"

"Then the Arab gave you the money because you. . . . What did you do?"

"I did nothing. Really nothing. I only opened

171

the garden door. The girls were willing. In fact I could have had pay from them if I were that sort of person. But I am not. . . . But you won't send me back!"

Now the girls came into the room fresh and gay. Their bodies had been steamed pink and curry-combed, Roman fashion, with flexible horn scrapers. But the cool pool had brought back the stark whiteness to their skins. Their hair was tied up in tight knots on top and they were dressed in bath gowns supplied by the matron, but these were too large for their slight figures. This formed the substance of their first complaint.

"Look, Do-do, what terrible gowns they gave us!"

"What did you call me?" asked Pilate.

"Do-do. It's a nice name."

Then another spoke. "Really it is nice."

"But what does it mean?"

"Nothing. No name means anything."

"Well, I thought it was a kind of Greek fish."

"Oh, no. How could you think such a thing? Really Do-do is a nice name and we all like it. Don't we like it?"

172

"Yes, we do," they all spoke together.

They settled themselves about his feet and continued.

"But look at these terrible gowns. They are built for two."

"Don't listen to them, Governor," interrupted Zozo. "They could confuse seven sages and their endless chatter could drive a whole army into disorder."

"That will do from you," said Buncha. "Come out of here, you black son of a rat. Come with me." Then turning to Pilate she said; "When man and woman are alone they can better know each other's thoughts."

With these words she led Zozo into another room and sat down opposite him.

She held her key in hand and said; "Not one word from you."

"But I must tell you that . . ."

She tapped him smartly on the knee. "Not one word!"

"But . . ."

She pecked him again. "I heard enough. Not one word."

He grumbled under his breath and was silent. He fingered nervously the golden chain of twisted links about his neck.

She sat there looking at him until he wished he had been under the ground. When he took a deep breath and opened his mouth as though about to speak she held the key aloft and he held back his words.

After a time he could stand it no longer and he cried out; "Beat me if you like but I must talk."

"Well if you must you must. But say something sensible."

He hesitated. "Well," he began. "I have decided to give you half."

"Half of the money?"

"Yes."

And as he put his hand to his belt to undo the purse she let the key out again and clawed his hand across the knuckles.

"What do you want from me?" he whined, blowing his warm breath on his fingers.

"In time you will learn your place. Not one more word from you."

The big black negro who only a short time be-

174

fore had strutted into the palace with pride and swagger was now cowed and squirmed in his seat before a small, only-up-to-his-waist, stubby female Babylonian dwarf. He watched the large wooden key that had metal teeth with a worried look.

In the other room the girls, whose silliness could divert a whole herd of elephants from the course of their stampede, were carrying on in the following manner.

"But really, Do-do, see how big these wraps are. They are so unbecoming and you will think. . . ."

The youngest took up the conversation; "Yes, you will think we are fat."

"But we are not. Are we?"

"No," said one.

"Oh, no," said the second.

"See, of course not," said the third, and she showed her knee and thigh.

"The matron will order new ones to be sewn," said Pilate.

"And Do-do, let mine be red. I love red."

"And mine also."

"And mine," added the third. "I like gay things."

"And Do-do," began the first. "If this is to be

our room then we should have a fresh floor. This
floor is old."

"But it's still good," protested Pilate.

"Good it is," said the eldest. "But it is not nice."

"And it is broken and the clay is damp."

"Yes, Do-do. We want a floor with those green
stones hammered into it."

"Like the floor around the pool," added her
charming sister.

"You mean a floor made of small malachite stones
pounded into hard clay?"

"Yes and with the little red berries here and
there."

"Those are not berries. They are bits of coral."

"Oh, is that what it is!"

"Yes, that is what we would like."

"But my dear children," said Pilate. "Where can
we get the malachite?"

"Oh, Do-do. You do not have to get it yourself.
You could order it."

"Yes, yes. I believe I could. There are several
malachite columns in a building not far off and we
could break them up. I will see to it myself."

"There!" They clapped their hands.

176

"Good." said one.

And the eldest put her arm around his neck and added; "Do-do will do everything for us, won't he?" and she looked seriously into his watery blue eyes.

"And now," began Pilate. "Tell me the truth. Who sent you here and who brought you?"

"They were nice, weren't they? But we don't know them at all."

"You know, Do-do. They were in such a terrible hurry we are all shaken up. I thought the flesh would come off our bones."

"Yes, they were nice," added the third, "very nice and very fast but also very slow."

"They hardly looked at us once. Oh, I was so bored! And I do not like them at all."

"And you know, Do-do. You owe us each a bracelet."

"A bracelet!" cried Pilate. "By the gods of thunder how do I owe you each. . . ."

"Now Do-do. You must not swear."

"Oh, he is so nice," said the second. "I don't care if he does swear."

And the third explained; "We saw such a won-

derful beggar that we had each to throw him a
bracelet."

"Another mountain preacher!" growled Pilate.

"No he wasn't, Do-do."

"He was sick and crawled out of his cave like a
cat and he spoke so beautifully."

"What did he say?"

"He told fortunes."

"Oh, sister, it was not fortunes."

"What was it then? He gave the past and the
future."

"True," said the eldest. "He recited about the
whole world and it was really beautiful."

"But what did he say?" asked Pilate.

"He said everything was to become so evil."

"And it was really lovely, Do-do. And we gave
him the bracelets from you."

"From me!"

"Yes," reasoned the eldest. "As you receive us
with all our trappings; this all comes to you as from
heaven. Now how should you know that we are
each of us missing a bracelet. We must tell you and
explain how it comes to be missing. Surely you
could not expect us to lose . . ."

178

"And Do-do," quickly interrupted the youngest, "you could put it down on a tablet as a necessary expense of the journey."

"Most necessary," said the second.

"It was one like this," said the first, showing the rings on her ankle. "Look Do-do, like this one, not round but a little oval. Our feet are too small for the round ones. Here take this one with you so that . . ." She removed a ring from her foot and put it into his hand.

"I suppose," Pilate said, "if I only allowed it you would put this ring through my nose and with a cord you would lead me around."

"Oh, no, Do-do. How can you say such a thing!"

"Of course not, Do-do. We have not asked for a single thing and we have now been here for quite a while."

"A long time," added the youngest.

"Do-do is joking with us," concluded the third, and they laughed and clapped their hands.

"Now we know how he jokes without even smiling. It is so funny."

"Say it again, Do-do. Tell us again about the ring through your nose."

"No, let him alone, sister. He does not want to say it again."

"Now I think I could recite," said the youngest.

"You had your chance before."

"Yes. I want to make a rhyme. Something about Do-do and the old flip-flap."

"No!" protested the eldest. "You forget that you are a lady."

"I am a lady too. I will compose it later. To-morrow I will show it to you Do-do."

And after a short pause the eldest began in a serious way; "And you know Do-do, what would be oh, so nice. . . ."

"Stop!" he cried. "It is enough for one day."

With these words he left the room and Buncha, seeing Pilate come into the hallway, tucked the key into her belt and skipped after him.

As soon as the female dwarf had gone, Zozo ran to the girls and sank on his knees before them.

"Save me! Save me!" he cried, with tears in his eyes. "Save me from that packed-up frog of a devil! She is like nothing human and one half of her is more than enough for the whole wide world! She wants to kill me, one finger at a time. Save me!"

"Poor Zozo," said the eldest. She took his hand and patted the tears on his black cheeks with the sleeve of her loose robe. "Poor Zozo."

And the others chimed in; "Poor Zozo. Poor Zozo."

Now and then, a woman in the quarters, under some pretext or other, would wander through the hall to catch a jealous glance of the new arrivals. The Greek girls seeing them pass would screw up their faces and stick out their saucy tongues.

When Pilate and Buncha came into the long hall the Babylonian dwarf asked; "And what did you find out?"

"What did I find out! Nothing! They are overflowing with babbling gibberish!"

"Really, not a thing?"

"No. In fact I know even less now than I did before. But of one thing I feel certain and that is that the Arab who brought them was no servant of Ben Rashid. The girls did not seem to know him. What do you say now, Buncha?"

"You get no information out of them? Well, that is good. And they are white as snow."

"Even whiter. Now, what is your verdict?"

181

"I say that the girls must remain. But for some strange reason we have become receivers of stolen wares."

"True. True. But what is to be done? Ben Rashid will soon know his loss and he will cry loud and long. He may even bring suit in the court of justice."

"It is simple" said the dwarf. "Write him at once. Write him with style and flourish and thank him for the magnificence of his gift. At the same time praise him as a loyal subject, which he knows he is not. But he dare not deny this loyalty any more than he will dare protest against the present."

Pilate smiled; "Buncha, without your wits, Judea would be a place intolerable."

And so it was done. The letter was prepared with "style and flourish," and sent to Cæsarea by a special courier instructed to deliver it with great ceremony and pomp.

XII

"Stop the Arab with the young Jew!" The chariots set out with all possible speed from the barracks beneath the Temple. Shouts echoed from wall to wall, and the archers, the spear-men, the cavalry charioteers, stone-slingers and the heavy guards in charge of the battering-rams and other engines of war, all demanded what was going on. The confusion among them only added to the uproar.

And Sulla too, deep in the dungeon with a crust of bread and a jar of water, he too heard the shouts.

"It's the same! It's the same!" he cried. "Let me out and I will get at them! Let me out!" He shook the chains that held the gate.

"Hey, there you. Keep quiet!" shouted a guard.

"Tell them to let me out before it is too late. I could recognize these two in the dark. Myself I will take them and with my own hands I will strangle them."

"Keep quiet!"

"They are the same. They are mine! Let me at them! Oh, Mars, break my chains and let me get them myself! Hurl down your thunderbolt to help me. Deliver them into my hands! Oh! Oh!" he screamed. "Let me out!"

He banged the chains but they held firm and when his violence was spent, he drank some water and, panting for breath, threw himself on the straw to plot, to plan, to scheme those scenes of murderous torture and revenge for which his soul ached. Nothing seemed terrible enough, no horrors cruel enough to pay for his mortification and ruin. He dreamed beautiful dreams of imaginary, impossible revenge and he called upon the gods to help him. To destroy his two enemies was not enough; and to stamp upon their bodies was also not sufficient; they must be crushed into the ground, so that not a trace of their former selves remained, and the stain! . . . Yes, even that had to be pounded away.

But while he cried behind his bars, Barzor and Rongus arrived safely in Bethlehem.

The four chariots raced on to Herodium and other places before the bewildered drivers abandoned the pursuit and turned slowly homeward in the evening with horses weary and spent.

The gray-headed Yaba met his master and together they entered the city.

"The litters?" asked Yaba.

"We cut them down but all else is safe."

"And the document?"

"That we bring with us."

"Good."

"And what is new, Yaba?"

"Everything is in order. And for us all is well in Judea."

They walked on and as they walked the old Arab turned to Rongus and said; "You might like to hear a little news yourself. The young people are waiting for you."

"You mean the blind boy and his sister?" He could have shouted for joy.

"Yes. My black slave found them and they are waiting."

"In the house?" Rongus asked anxiously.

"Yes. But they would not enter before they had a rabbi come and place a charm beside the door. They are strict in their faith. The girl says that they must leave tomorrow and continue their search."

"That I know," explained Rongus. "She seeks a certain prophet who can perform miracles."

"It's nonsense," answered the old Arab. "My head is gray and I have seen many prophets and I tell you again—all their miracles are only sorcery. They are stuffed with falsehood and their words are empty wind."

They reached the gate of the house and the weary camels were tied in the yard.

Rongus opened the neck of his shirt so that part of the golden armor would show and stood before the blind beggar and his sister.

"I knew it wasn't true," she said. Then she took hold of her brother's hand and said to him. "He is here now. The one who saved you from the rushing horses."

The blind boy kneeled down and raising his clasped hands prayed to God that all blessings might come "to those who lead me in my darkness."

"Yes, I wanted so much to tell you it wasn't true. I wanted to. . . . Well, I am glad you are found. I am very glad!"

"And I, too, never had a chance fully to thank you for my brother David and for myself."

"What is your name?" asked Rongus simply.

"I am called Mariamne. But we are orphans and we have nobody."

"Your people are all dead?"

"Yes! Killed by the son of Herod."

"Well, at least they did not sell you into slavery," he said.

"I think David would have been sold, if illness had not burnt out his sight."

"Do you know," said Rongus, "it seems very strange; I am also without parents, but I have an uncle, may his soul rot!"

"Don't say that. You should not talk like that."

"Well, I must explain. . . ." He sat down before them and, weary as he was, he recited all the main events of his life from the time his uncle sold him

to the Romans to the day that Marcus Sulla arrived
at the quarry and Barzor bought him, as he stood
tied up at the stake of punishment in the barracks
yards. He told them his name and how his present
master had given him the golden breast-plate and
about the promise that Barzor had made . . . the
promise that he would soon be free.

The brother and sister listened with deep attention and suddenly the eyes of the girl filled—she
could not hold back any longer—the tears streamed
down her cheeks. And her blind brother suspected
that she was weeping silently and put his fingers
gently up to her streaming eyes and the three sat
quietly together in happy friendship. Then Rongus
took her hand in his.

Barzor from the other room, changing his
clothes and washing the sand of Cæsarea and the
dust of Jerusalem from his hands and face, heard
some of the words that were spoken. He heard
Mariamne tell Rongus that Antipas, the cruel son
of Herod, had killed their parents and when he
heard this tale his heart was touched; he lived again
through the never-forgotten tragedy of his own
life.

But now Yaba interrupted his thoughts. "You have the document safe?" asked the old Arab.

"Yes, here."

The old man unrolled the parchment and inspected the seal. His eyes brightened. "It is good. It is excellent!" he said.

"Now bring me a razor," said Barzor when he finished his toilet.

The razor was stropped on a bit of skin and when it was keen it was handed to Barzor.

And while the blind youth David and his sister Mariamne together with Rongus were relating fragments of their own lives and shedding tears for each other in sympathy and understanding—Barzor unrolled the parchment in the other room and, beginning at the top, scraped away the writing, line by line, until not a single word remained except the signature of Pilate and the wax seal beside it, stamped with the official crest from his ring. The parchment was plucked clean of its words, like a bird of its feathers, and now it lay fresh and blank before them. . . . Upon it could now be written the all-important lines for which they schemed and dared and risked so much.

189

XIII

THAT night when Pilate was informed that the chariots had returned to Jerusalem after an unsuccessful chase, he cried out; "A wretched Arab and a boy Jew, and our fastest horses and picked soldiers are helpless! Are our legions nanny-goats? Have I no Romans here? What do they eat to weaken them so! They sell their candles in the market places, I know, I know, and they sit in the dark. But have they sold their manhood too! And they call for wine! Wine from Rome! Wine for worthless ninny-flits! Send for the captains! Bring them here at once! By Jupiter, I will have those two—if I must send the whole legion into the wilderness to find them. I will bring legion twenty, *Valeria!* who are now in Syria! What are we here, bath-rubbers dressed in cotton armor!" He raged and in his heat and temper he paced the hall until the captains appeared hurriedly before him.

He walked along the line, then he turned his back to the officers and bit his lips. Suddenly he faced about; "Only the veterans!" he shouted and set his jaw.

He turned to the end of the line and lifting each metal guard attached to the brass helmet rubbed his hand on the soldier's chin and drew forward only those who had hardened flesh under their jaws. Here were the picked veterans and no records were needed to prove their service. The rest were sent back to the barracks, much disturbed by the anger of Pilate and the recent strange happenings.

Then Pilate began again to repeat what he said before they arrived and once more he threatened to displace their troops with "the Boars," as the twentieth legion was sometimes called, because its standards carried this emblem.

Still raging, Pilate now heaped alternate abuse

191

and encouragement on his veterans. "These thieves must be caught. There is trouble brewing all around. If you cannot get them I will send you back to Rome."

And while he scolded them, Sulla in the dungeon, hearing of the failure of the pursuit, cried out again; "Let me out! I will deliver them to you! Alone I will take them and drag their bodies before you! Let me out!"

That night the captains sent scouts south to Bethlehem, Etam, Nephtoah and as far as Herodium while some went north and east as far as Bethel and Jericho, and still others were placed on watch about the walls of Jerusalem. Three soldiers were stationed on the hill of Calvary just outside the north wall and three at the southern arch, the Dung Gate. Two spear-men guarded the breach in the south wall made by the unfinished aqueduct and six patrolled the wooded grove of Gethsemane just east of the Temple and across a small ravine. Their activity was tremendous.

But Pilate was in a fit of fury and paced up and down the long hall of columns and growled; "Legions of bearded nanny-goats! Daisy-trotters!

Kissing love-birds! Are there no Romans amongst them?"

And the female Babylonian dwarf skipped after him and piped out; "It will do them good. That's what they need. Go on. Don't stop. Let loose the demons! Who is governor here in Judea? Are you a governor for nothing?"

"No, Buncha. Now is their time to learn. They will learn now that the governor is a Roman, and if they do not know what a Roman is like, I will show them."

"Yes. That is what is coming to them. They are all soft. They sell their allowance of candles for a few pennies. Then they sit in the dark and drink *posca*. Now they can learn who is the governor sent by our Imperator Tiberius Cæsar from Rome. And what is Rome is Rome. Oh, they will learn, they will learn. Even if their ears were on their backsides they will hear everything."

"Is there not trouble enough without this? Judea a nest of hornets! And Antipas, that sick, weak-minded son of Herod, for a king, who does nothing and knows nothing. A pack of black-scheming priests who hoard the coins that they squeeze from the devout. A mad populace who set up the cry of 'Graven Image!—Tear down the false gods of Imagery!' and thousands shouting these words, clamor upon the walls and destroy the standards and golden eagles of Cæsar. They trample them under foot! Every day a new fanatic cries out that he is king of the Jews and there are some who would believe it. And every night there are disturbances and secret meetings and dark plottings, every one against the other. The priests against the Romans, the feeble king against the people and the people against all three. And the whole hotbed can be described in one word; Judea!"

He walked rapidly up and down and the female dwarf skipped after him.

But he had hardly finished these last words when one of the pages came into the room and announced that Caiaphas, the high priest of the Temple, had come with six other priests on a matter of great importance.

"Send for the secretaries. I must have witness. Let them come at once for I will not hold speech with these holy dogs unless the words are marked down in writing. From one day to the next they would deny their own mothers. Bring the secretaries first."

The page ran through the halls of the Towers to do as he was ordered.

"What can they want?" asked Pilate.

"Whatever it is, they come at a bad time," replied the dwarf.

"If it is bad for us, it will also be bad for them. When the gods shower misfortune, they scatter wide."

"Good. This is no time to come here anyway."

Soon the secretaries arrived and took their places at the small marble desks along the wall. They lit tall candles and made themselves ready.

Slowly, and as one man, the priests came forward. They were dressed in costly silks, fringed with heavy gold embroidery and jewels were about their necks and on their fingers. Their beards were curled and the long curls stiffly varnished with costly ointments. A pungent odor of myrrh hung like a dank cloud about them. Their manner was threatening and unpleasant.

"The hour is late," said Pilate smiling.

"It is important. Otherwise we should not have come. We want our holy vestments."

"I see."

"We want them at once."

"Not so hasty my good friends."

"They belong to us and we need them."

"Tonight?"

"Yes. At once. Together with the sacred vessels and the jewelled breast-plate."

"Is that all you require?"

"We want only what is ours and has always been ours."

"And I suppose you have another holy service tomorrow?"

"Every day and every service is holy to us."

"No. That will not do. Your vestments and sacred relics together with your breast-plate are locked up and are safer here with me than in your Temple."

"My child may be safer with you but still it is my child and you cannot keep him away from me."

"Please speak plainly. Say exactly what you want."

"We have already told you. We require the

196

prayer shawls and the golden vessels. You have agreed to give them to us on the days we require them. We have your word—your oath."

"Yes. I have promised. You shall have them on your holy days for your services. You have my word for it but tomorrow is not a day that you hold sacred."

"We need them tonight!"

"You do not need them until next week, the end of next week."

"We did not come here for religious instruction."

"But it is so. Your holy days of Passover do not arrive until the end of next week."

"We are to listen to you and you will inform us when our Passover should take place and what happy day we are to choose for the atonement of our beloved dead! You rule us in body and now you would have our souls also."

"Nonsense. Give me none of your quibbles. You are here for something. Say plainly what you want. You ask for holy vestments. Yes, I have them. They are safe under lock and key. They belong to you. No one questions it."

"Then release them. We are here to carry them back."

"But not so fast. You will not talk plainly. Why do you need the vestments when your holy services do not start for another week or more? Why? Will you answer this?"

"They are necessary. They need to be gone over and cleaned."

"We do not use them and they have not been soiled."

"In religious matters we cannot follow your instruction."

"Well then if you will not talk to the point I will tell you openly what you probably already imagine. The vessels are yours. No one denies it. The vestments, the prayer shawls and the jewelled breast-plate, all are yours. If you hold these objects in reverence that is your own concern and Cæsar will not meddle with your beliefs. I keep them here not because they are unsafe in your Temple but because they are the symbols of your power and that power is sometimes not a good one. For your holy days, for your altar and for your services, I give you all the objects your religion requires; but

198

on other days you do not need them and you cannot have them. . . ."

The high priests consulted among themselves in whispering tones.

Then Caiaphas stepped a little forward. "Why?" he said. And, behind him the other six priests repeated together; "Why?"

"Why? I have already told you. Your influence with the people is great only when you are robed in the holy garments, when you hold before them the traditional vessels of their religion, when they see the golden, jewelled plaque on your breast. On holy days, you may not, by the laws of your race, engage in warfare but on other days what is to stop you from putting on your sacred robes and leading the whole populace against your Roman rulers? What will hold you back from such an attempt?"

"We are holy men."

"Ha, ha! I laugh in your faces. Holy—you call yourselves. Holy for what?"

"Blasphemer!"

"Holy for what? You are no more holy than a pig. You will understand that, won't you? I did not say a sheep or a goat. I said . . . Ha, ha! And you call it holy to gather in the animals for sacrifice and sell them for double and triple their worth? This is holy. And about the pigeon breeding in the yards. . . . This is also holy. And the treasure that you concealed from me, you hid it away so that we could not build the aqueduct. You did not want fresh water to come into Jerusalem. And now you stand before me and call yourselves holy men. Yes, and you lied to me. You said you had no gold and no silver only a few miserable bags! But the soldiers rooted out the chests. Holy men do not lie! And the money-changers in the open court. . . ."

"What about them, Roman Blasphemer?

"Are they not working together with you holy men!"

"You insult us!" They drew closer together.

"Will you deny it? How is it then that there are no small coins on the tables? Do you not hold them back? Why are your small coins sold for double their worth? Because you would rather have the larger ones from those who come to worship in the Temple. Why will you allow no money but coins of your own mintage to enter the gates?

Are the Roman coins worthless? Our silver is tin, and our gold is brass in your eyes!"

"You know the reason, unholy tyrant. You know very well that no face or figure, no graven image may appear in our sacred grounds. Our belief strictly forbids imagery, and those who worship figures and idols and golden calves are outcasts."

"I do not ask you to worship our money. I merely ask you to accept it."

"Never! Never! Never! No graven image shall ever profane our holy Temple! Never!"

"And what revenue do you get from the money-changers? Between you and these corrupt agents you manage to bleed your people. Why? Because you like to call yourselves holy men and come here. . . ."

Again Caiaphas advanced, his face twitching with anger. "Enough! We did not come here to be insulted; we came here for a definite purpose. We want our vestments. Will you give them to us or will you not?"

Silent and almost motionless the secretaries at their desks wrote down every spoken word, and they also wrote down Pilate's replies. Buncha, the dwarf, sat with them in the shadow.

"You have already had my answer. You may have them at the end of next week when you actually need them for your services, not sooner."

"We need them tonight."

"It is not true."

"Then if we must give you a reason you will have it. We need seven days to purify the robes and vessels; they have been polluted by your defiling hands."

"I never even touched them."

"No matter. They have been in your house."

"Yes. And they will remain here until. . . . Last year and the year before and on every other occasion, a day before your holiday was sufficient time to make holy again your sacred things. Why do you now need seven?"

"Because the evil is greater. Because our most learned and revered elders have debated this subject for weeks and this is their conclusion. And what our wise men decide let no fool mock!"

"And if you think I am a fool you should think

again. The vestments are here; and here they will remain until next Friday. I am no fool. The pilgrims are arriving in flocks, the roads are filled with travellers coming to Jerusalem. They will sleep in the streets and on the roofs—everywhere. The population will be swollen to six or eight times their number. The wild mountain preachers are stirred up against you holy men of the Temple and there are the mad prophets and rogues and thieves that need to be watched. And while—Oh no, I am not the fool you think. . . . While our soldiers are occupied, in ten directions, you will put on the badge of your authority and lead a mob against me here in the Towers because—because I have taken your money to build the waterway and because I know that you are in league with the changers and because I know your other scheming tricks. Holy men or demons, be what you may, but no vestments! No!"

"This then is your decision," answered the high priest, holding back with all the strength that was in him a torrent of angry words.

"Final!"

"Then we are to return empty-handed?" His

hands were clenched and the pitch of his voice was over-strung.

"Yes."

"And will you be ready to stand by the events that may result from your refusal?"

"Ready—Yes, we are ready!"

"We will not be responsible."

"May good luck go with you," replied Pilate with mock cheerfulness, concluding the interview.

Slowly they withdrew in brooding silence, but before they reached the steps Caiaphas, the high priest, turned for a final thrust.

"You forget, Roman," he said, pointing his trembling finger to the ground. "You forget that these are Our people and this Our land."

XIV

Barzor and Rongus changed their clothes for beggar's rags, soiled their faces with tanner's oil and, staining their hands with indigo, prepared to set out to meet the armed caravan coming from Rome with the treasure for the Temple. The stain on their hands and faces proved to all that they were two travelling dyers. But underneath the rags and cords that tied them together, Rongus wore his golden breast-plate. From this he could not be parted.

While the crouching camels were being prepared for the journey, Mariamne came quietly into the yard.

"When you return we shall probably be gone," she said.

His face fell. "Why must you go so soon?" Rongus asked and there was a feminine rise in his voice.

"We seek the one who performs the miracles."

"Ehi!" exclaimed the white-headed Arab, screwing up his face. "It is all make-believe sorcery."

"It is not to us. We believe, and we must seek until we find."

"Wait over until we return, then you shall tell me all about him and then I too may have something important to say." Rongus spoke these words softly.

"Nothing is important to me unless David can get back his sight."

"Wait only a day or so and then perhaps I may be free and together we shall go and seek this healer. . . . Anywhere you like we will go."

She looked at him with her full sad eyes but did not reply.

"Wait, we shall not be long," he pleaded.

"Long enough," she said, and shook her head slowly. "Besides," she added, "there are things going on here that I cannot understand. Why are you and Barzor so disguised?"

"I cannot tell you now Mariamne. You must trust us. Everything can be explained."

"How long will you be gone?"

"Only about two days and then we shall be back."

She hesitated and then consented to remain. A happy thought came to her mind. "We have a few pennies and I will find a Hebrew teacher in Bethlehem and bring him here to teach David the Proverbs from the holy books. He has had lessons from time to time."

"Good. Let him come at once. We shall not be gone long."

In the meantime Barzor had taken the jar containing Cleopatra's spices and, wrapping it carefully in a cloth, tied it to the saddle on the camel's back. Soon all was ready. Yaba and his black slave opened the gate for them and with a casual salute they started off.

Mariamne stood in the narrow street and watched them until they turned the corner and were out of sight.

The main streets through which they passed buzzed with noise, and the two men caught snatches of the talk as they passed along. The people were suspicious of the newly arrived Roman soldiers but they assured each other that it was not for a tax on fruit. There were rumors that "two rich Arabs riding in littered camels" were being sought. Barzor and Rongus laughed silently. Sometimes the gossip became "two Arabs" and nothing was said of the young Jew.

As they passed through the gate of the wall they saw several of the Roman spear-men standing guard. One of them even raised his spear and called; "Get on there. Don't loiter here at the gate!"

They turned the heads of the camels northwards.

When they were well upon the road Rongus said; "Master, some day I shall have my freedom."

"You are more free with me than you could ever be by yourself."

"Really it is almost too free."

"Well, if you so desire. But why do you ask?"

"No special reason. I only wanted to tell Mariamne how long she should wait."

"Oh, I see. And what will you do when you are free?"

"I don't know but I shall go with them to seek what they seek and watch over them."

"And beg for your bread?"

"No. I shall rent a square of land and work it and we shall live first in a tent before I can haul up enough clay for a house."

"I see you have already made plans for the future."

"I shall ask Mariamne to marry me. I would have done so this morning, if I had only known how long it would be."

"When we get back you can say that you will be released in a few days. By the end of the week certainly."

"Good. You make me very happy and I do not know what I have done to deserve it."

"Rongus, I have liked you from the start. It is quite strange but when I look into your face I am reminded of long ago. . . . Of things that were once so close to me. . . . Of my wife and the little child and the days when I was a happy man, and wished good for all."

They drove on. To the left about a league away they saw the broken walls of Jerusalem and soon they were beyond this holy city on the road to Jericho and the valley of the river Jordan.

Here and there along the road Roman soldiers were stationed keeping a sharp lookout for "the Arab and the young Jew dressed in silks."

They used this order as a pretext to stop pilgrims and other travellers along the road. Their manner was rude and overbearing and their voices gruff. They detained only those who seemed to have something in their packs and who would probably be willing to pay a little to be allowed to proceed without delay. But those who had nothing were not bothered.

Several times on the road, soldiers stopped Barzor and Rongus and poked their hands in the packs, but these bundles contained little besides the bare necessities for several days journey and the old clay jar filled with some evil-smelling spices.

In the section of Judea through which they passed, the cross-roads and valley passes were filled with spies and agents employed by Antipas, the feeble son of Herod, and the high priest of the

Temple to watch and report all movements of the numerous mountain preachers, the self-appointed prophets and other fanatics who gathered disciples about them and stirred up the people with cries of rebellion. These watchers, provided with plenty of money, would come in from their posts and meet in the neighboring inns for good evening meals, grape-wine and noisy talk. They worried and cursed the innkeepers; they almost came to blows with the Roman soldiers and they quarrelled with each other. While the Roman soldiers were only gruff in their manner, these agents of Antipas were provokers and inciters so base that no ugliness was beneath them.

In this green strip of land, with sloping fields and clear refreshing streams flowing in its valley, ready to quench the thirst of the hot arid desert, here was the joyous cradle of a future civilization; but here also at this time stood the spike-like sentinels—the spies and oppressors of Antipas and the coarse Roman cleavers of peace.

"But Judea will be free," Barzor kept saying to himself. "Free from the evil priests and the heavy yoke of Rome."

At sundown they rested and refreshing them-selves with food and water set off again before it was fully dark to force their journey through the night. And at the first glimpse of dawn they were leagues and leagues away from Jerusalem.

In a small town they found a miller's shed and two girls on the ground turning the stones of the small hand mills. Here they bought four bags of fresh corn and went on to a place in the desert where they knew the caravan from Rome must pass.

While waiting for the caravan to arrive they undid the sacks of corn. Into each they mixed a handful of the pungent spices from the jar. These were the spices that fell many years before from the bandages wrapped around the dead body of Cleopatra that had been placed with the relics in Herod's tomb. They threw away the empty jar and turned the bottom of the sacks up several times to churn the contents thoroughly.

At noon the caravan came into sight. Forty-four camels—six had died during the long journey—a troop of Romans armed with swords and cross-bows, the merchants in charge, a few pilgrims journeying to the Holy City under the protection of this strong force, several women and children being sent home with safe escort and two Roman officers who rode ahead with the chief navigator and captain of the caravan. The treasure itself was contained in small oak boxes, nailed with leather bands and sealed with rosin. Because of the heavy weight of the bullion, two of these boxes were sufficient load for a camel and only half the animals of the caravan were treasure-laden, the rest carried those members of the train privileged to ride and the provisions necessary for man and beast.

Barzor and Rongus kneeled by the roadside and awaited the long marching file.

"Peace! Peace be with you," they bowed low.

The Roman captains and chiefs of the caravan stopped to examine these two whose hands and faces clearly showed what they were—travelling dyers.

"We have been robbed of our money and we have only grain for our beasts and a little silver. Here, so much." With these words Barzor showed a few coins in his hand.

"Well what do you want?"

"Peace be with you. We ask only protection. We will pay. The four bags of feed are yours if we may be allowed to follow you for two days and two nights."

"And your destination?"

"We are bound for Jericho where there is much leather to be tanned and we should arrive before the holidays."

"Good. Join in behind and give the bags to the camel boys. In two days we should reach Bethel and there you leave us and take the road to the left."

"To the left?" Barzor asked, pretending innocence.

"Yes. We will direct you," the navigator replied, starting on.

Barzor and Rongus took their places humbly at the end of the long line. They made friends at once with the bored camel-boys. The bags of feed were given over to them and Barzor addressed a word to them. He told the boys that the officers said that all the grain was to be used in the evening.

That night the forty-four feed buckets were filled with grain and fed to the camels.

At the first glimpse of dawn a horrible sight was before all. Forty-four camels lay dead in the sand! Their legs were drawn under them as though in convulsion. And their glassy eyes were open and rolled upwards. A film of fine sand, blown by the breeze, covered their unblinking eyeballs. And the pink of their mouths was already a purplish blue. Stone dead! And nothing could stir them.

The great treasure with its strong guard and escort, with all its boxes nailed and sealed with rosin, and its troop of cross-bow men, who had nothing to shoot, all were now trapped, leagues from the nearest point of aid, in a desert sand.

Barzor and Rongus were not with them.

XV

When this terrible thing was discovered all became panic and confusion.

"Unstrap the boxes!" ordered the Roman captains. "Bring them all here and prepare to stand guard!"

"No, not here," suggested the navigator. "Better some distance away, on the little mound. There is too much dead flesh in this spot and besides we will have a better view from the top."

The captains agreed. The boxes were moved to the top of the sand mound. The saddles were saved and also the provisions and water.

"We may expect an attack at any moment. Let us not be found unprepared," said one.

"This is the work of an Arab band," added another.

"We are lost. We are lost," wailed the women. And the children were frightened and cried. The soldiers formed into a hollow square and camped beside the treasure. One of the Roman captains removed his helmet and breast-plate and other encumbering trappings and taking a staff in hand set out on foot accompanied by two spear-men in the direction of the nearest city. This they were unable to reach until night and, as the gates were closed, they were forced to wait until dawn before they could enter the city.

Now they secured camels and drove on for the whole day, reaching Bethel only in time to enter before the gates closed for the night. At Bethel they found Roman soldiers who gave them chariots and fast horses and when the gates opened at dawn they made the short dash to Jerusalem and went straight to the Towers.

"Forty-four dead! And the treasure trapped in the sand!" cried Pilate.

"We are three days away and by this time the raid may already have taken place. Send us more troops at once and camels to bring in what remains."

"Are you certain it is an Arab trick?" asked Pilate.

"Yes. They were dressed in rags and pretended to be dyers. Their hands were blue."

"Both were Arabs?"

"No. The younger was a Jew! But his arms and legs showed muscles of great strength."

"It is they! The same! I wager my life it is the two. . . . Here, send for the captains! Let them come at once with all possible speed!"

And Buncha pulled at Pilate's purple toga and said; "It can be no other. It is the same two."

"And did they show you a paper of safe conduct signed and sealed by myself?"

"No, they carried nothing only the grain and they showed a few coins of silver."

"And did the old one have a dagger concealed?"

"We did not notice."

"And under the rags did the young Jew have plate?"

218

"We did not see it."

"What did you see? Are you a captain or a stuffed doll?"

"The young one had black curly hair and the old one had a face hard and wrinkled."

"They are the same," interrupted Buncha. "But it is not the Temple treasure they are after."

"No? What then?"

"I do not know but it does not seem to be the Temple treasure."

"Why not?"

"I do not know but . . . Do not let the priests hear of it."

"Forty-four beasts dead. The treasure caught in the great waste and you say it is not. . ."

"It is not enough!" replied the Babylonian dwarf, standing as tall as she could to reach his ear.

"A whole caravan of gold and silver and it is not enough!"

"That is what I say."

"What then! What more!"

She shook her head and shrugged her shoulders for she had no words for reply. In a moment the captains appeared from the barracks.

"Sound the horns, call the troops! The treasure from Rome has been trapped in the desert. Let them go forward at once. Do not delay!"

The captain of the caravan who had come into Jerusalem with this news ran out together with those whom Pilate ordered. They crossed the stone arch and dashed into the barracks.

The bugles sounded.

Buncha said; "Whatever the plan, keep it silent. Let not the priests of the Temple learn that the treasure. . . ."

"No, no. By no means. They must not know for they will suspect. Whatever happens the treasure must be saved, even if it takes a whole army! Think of it! A whole army of Romans for two flea-jumpers! Spare nobody! Spare nothing! Let no two stones rest together unmoved. Turn everything upside down but bring them here before me!"

"Do not leave yourself unprotected," warned the dwarf.

"True, Buncha, you speak wisely." His voice was softened, and now he whispered; "There may be a hidden trick."

220

Then he sent for his Latin secretaries and dictated a message, in the presence of all the officers and soldiers in the hall, that was to go forward by night and day with all speed possible, to bring without delay the Syrian troops into Jerusalem.

"Is there nobody who can rid us of these two!" he cried out. "Are we all eaters of grass and is there no one in the whole of Judea who can take them and bring them before me! Are you all suckling babes! What color blood is in you? Do you piss milk! Now I will make an oath before you all, and before all the gods, and the oath is this: If these two, whoever they may be, are not brought before me shortly, I will proclaim throughout the whole land, that, if they will come willingly I will make them officers with a rank above all our captains. I swear it; and I will do it! If they are so clever that none can take them, then I need them more than I need any of the rest. And they will be more worth to me than anyone here."

But now Sulla released from the dungeon and regardless of his dishevelled appearance, torn, soiled, and still aching in flesh and bone, ran breathlessly into the hall.

"I am here, your Excellency, and I have heard your oath. Myself, I will capture them. They shall pay me. I, only, can do it, for I, only, know them and their tricks," and he pointed to his toothless mouth. "And their dead bodies I will drag before you with a rope. Hercules himself could not hold me now! I go! It will be deeds and not words." He brandished his sword in fury.

"Go! Go! Out of my sight, you munching fool. Go!"

XVI

Safely within the little walled house in Bethlehem, now washed and clean, were Barzor and Rongus. Yaba the white-headed Arab was with them and also his black slave. In the next room beside a candlelight sat the blind boy David and his Hebrew teacher. And Mariamne heard the lesson.

"Repeat after me," said the unkempt teacher. His garments were soiled and torn. Then he read from a small scroll that was open before him.

"In three things a man's character can be recognized. First, in the wine-cup, secondly in his purse and finally in his anger."

The blind youth repeated the words of the scholar.

"Now say them again, so that they may fix themselves in your mind."

The boy said the lines over.

"Now tell me, David, how would you know if a man had been taking too much wine?"

"I could smell it. Or I could hear it by his loud or foolish words."

"Good. And how could you tell a man by his purse?"

"I could listen when he was bargaining or I could know how he pays out; whether it is slowly with fear and hesitation or promptly and recklessly. The coins themselves would clink and tell me."

"Good. And when he is angry you would know it by his words."

"And also if he were silent I would feel the heaviness of the air."

"Good. Now we will go on. Repeat after me: Men are like grass in the field; they grow up and wither away."

The youth repeated the lines.

"And you recall the lines from yesterday? What shortens life?"

"Envy, luxury and ambition."

"Correct. Now we will go on. Repeat: Our blood is no redder than the blood of our neighbors."

He said the proverb after his master.

"And now we have a little saying that is here recorded: The soldiers fight and the kings are heroes."

After the lad spoke these lines, the Hebrew scholar read a long page about virtue and the qualities of a wise man.

"Now," he concluded, "we can reduce all the virtues of a wise man to seven qualities. Listen carefully: A wise man does not speak first when a greater person is present. Two; he never interrupts anyone who is talking. Three; he does not answer hastily. Four; he speaks and replies in a modest manner. Five; he treats one thing after another in a proper order. Six; when he cannot answer he says quite frankly that he does not know. And seven; he acknowledges his mistakes without delay."

These words of ancient wisdom were repeated

225

several times before David fixed them in his mind.

"These are the qualities of a wise man. Now David, what would be the traits of a fool?"

"I don't know."

"Why, the opposite, of course."

"Yes, I understand."

"And what is the opposite of. . . ." Then he went over the lesson asking for the opposite of each quality and the boy gave the required answers.

"Now the opposite of virtue is sin," said the teacher. "And sin is an evil thing." He rolled the parchment to the required place and read aloud; "An evil impulse is at first delicate and thin as a spider's web, but soon it becomes strong as a cart rope. When evil is strong it is sin. Also you should know that evil committed with a good intent is better than a good work done from a wrong motive. And one thing more. Now if one does not consider an evil act a sin then is it a sin or is it not a sin?"

With these final words he began a long theological discussion and to display his learning he cited one authority after another.

But Mariamne did not follow the wandering

thread of his argument. Her thoughts were far away. Soon she left the room.

When the teacher saw that she was gone he drew nearer to David and quickly concluded his argument about sin.

"Now there is something written here that you must know." He cast a hasty glance about the room. "It is about women," he whispered with contempt. "In the book of laws it is written: 'If a woman brings her husband one female slave then she need not grind, bake or wash; if she brings her husband two slaves then she need not cook or suckle his child; if three, she need not make his bed or work in wool and if she brings four then she may sit in her chair of state.'"

He followed this with a dissertation on women, their virtues, but mainly their vices, and to illustrate his point he complained bitterly, with tears in his eyes, about his wife. "With her first child she lost all grace and charm, and nothing will bring it back. She sulks all day and the moment I appear she becomes quarrelsome. 'You will not divorce me,' she says. 'And I can throw all the salt in the soup that I like. Who will clean the house and wash the children and make the beds and feed your sour face? Who will do it for you? To hire people you need those little coins,' and she rubs her fingers together. 'You miserable fool; what have you got? A head stuffed with Hebrew jargon and no more sense to you than the letter *aleph*, and that upside-down.' This is what she tells me. And I say; 'You should have respect for learning. You must not laugh at it.' I reason with her and explain to her that wisdom stands close to God."

"What does she say to that?" asked David.

"She says; 'And the children have no sandals and can stand close to nothing; and they have no clothes and for shame must remain hidden; and they have no meat to eat and. . . . Stand a little further away from God, my good husband, and let us live like other people.' So you see my boy this is what it sometimes means to be a scholar, and a husband."

"But when you know everything," said David, and his face brightened, "then you are strong and you can do anything you like in the world. Knowledge is the greatest strength of all."

"Yes, yes. True. But with a wife like mine. . . . Now we must go on with our lesson. Here is writ-

ten some more about women," and he read from
the scroll; "A woman of sixty will run after music
like one of six."

In the other room the soft voice of Mariamne
came like notes of great peace and harmony. "You
are so good," she said, "but we would only hold
you back. We must take care of David."

"Of course we must. Where we live there will
be his home also and wherever we go, there will
he go, too."

"And Rongus, dear, I must seek for the
prophet—the true one, the good one—the one who
cures and when he cures it is not for a moment
nor for a day but it is for all time. Forever."

"As soon as I am free we will go together, and
together we will seek him and when we find
him. . . ."

"He will place his hand on David's head and,
Lo! behold! the whole world will appear before
him and he will be frightened by the sudden rush
of light and he will not know the strange faces
about him. But I will take him quickly in my arms
and kiss him and say; 'Here I am. This is your sister
Mariamne and you are her only and dearest, dear-

est brother. Oh, David! This sudden blaze that you see before you is only the outside world.' "

"Then what would be his first words?"

"I don't know Rongus what they would be. I think there would be no words at all because the great things are the unseen and the unspoken. And if his eyes were open wide and he looked out upon a dazzling sight it would have nothing to do with the inside world that he already knows. No forms and colors can equal this feeling. The world where he knows I love him and he loves me. And the world in which great miracles happen."

The simple Rongus hardly understood. "But I love you too, Mariamne, and together we shall go and seek the one who can do this great thing."

"As soon as you have your liberty we shall go." She placed her hand in his and he pressed it tenderly.

"Next week it will certainly be. My master has given me his word. Next week or even sooner. That is not too long to wait, is it? And then everything can be explained."

"No, it is not long. But it is difficult to remain here when I feel that very close, very near, per-

haps only in the next street or at the city gate
stands the prophet who can . . . It is hard to
remain at rest with this thought, for peace will
never be in my heart until I find him."

"But you won't go off now when. . . . When
my master took me to Cæsarea, each night. . .
And now I fear you will go away and I shall lose
you again."

"Perhaps not."

"Then where could we meet if I ever lost you?"

"If I ever lost you, Rongus, darling, I would go
to the Holy City and there I would go to a holy
place. On the steps of the Temple court I would
stand and wait and wait—Oh, ever so long—until
you came. And you would come for me wouldn't
you?"

"Walls of cities and fortress chains could not
hold me back."

They were silent.

In the adjoining room they heard the voices of
David and the complaining scholar.

The teacher was reading from his scroll. "In
Palestine they say: Who is first silent in a quarrel
springs from a good family."

231

The boy repeated the words.

"Good. Now I will ask you something. If a man comes from a good family should he be proud?"

"Yes," replied David.

"Naturally we are all proud of our family, of our mother and our father. But man should not be too proud. It is not good. And do you know why God made man on the sixth day?"

"No."

"Well, for this very reason; in order that he should not be too proud, the little fly was created before him. When man is too proud he must perish; because when he is too proud he places himself above all law."

For a time he was silent, then he said; "Tell me David. What does it feel like to be blind?"

"I don't know."

"It is dark and everything black?"

"No."

"Then is it gray and do shadows move?"

"Yes. It is gray, shadows move and sometimes I think I can see a streak of light but I cannot make out if it runs up and down or crosswise. But often I feel it is just there—only around a little turning—Oh, so near, my hand could almost touch it."

"So it is, David. And soon, soon it will come. The Lord is good; He has mercy. Pray to the Lord, David, and He will open up the whole world before you."

With these remarks the lesson for the evening was concluded. The teacher rolled up his scroll and bade his pupil good-night.

As he passed through the hall of the house he bowed to Barzor and the old Arab Yaba who were seated at a table.

"Take care of the children of the poor," said the scholar. "From them will knowledge arise."

Barzor gave him a piece of gold money and tears came to the poor man's eyes. "The Lord should bless you a thousand times and may you prosper even more than you desire. As you see, I have nothing; we are poor. But when the gates of heaven are shut to prayers they are open to tears. Upon the poor children the great future depends. Take care of the children. Good-night. A thousand blessings."

With these words he bowed himself out of the door but he had not gone far when he came back and said; "There is a native magician; he once studied cures. He performs great wonders. Oh, such things, I could not begin to explain to you. Really marvellous. He drives out demons every day of the week. And he brings back reason on the Sabbath or any time he so wishes. As for diseases— he draws a sword and on the floor he places a chalk-line and he cries out; 'Stop!' And right there at the line it stops. Could you believe a thing like that? Well I was thinking. . . . I know where he lives and I could go there and arrange everything and then tomorrow night we might bring the blind boy there and see what he can do. The tail of a dead dog boiled in a pot performs wonders. Anyway let him try. Try this, try that, here, there, anywhere, and something will strike and there you will have it."

"If the boy's sister agrees you may make what arrangements are necessary," Barzor replied. "But I doubt if she will."

Again the poor teacher bowed himself out of the house.

Then Barzor said to Yaba.

"Better listen closely at the garden wall and

234

learn if the news has already been whispered abroad."

The old Arab went into the garden and in a minute he returned. The very thing that Pilate wanted kept strictly a secret was already on everyone's tongue, not alone in Jerusalem but also in Bethlehem.

Yaba reported; "They say the whole legion has been sent to the desert to capture the Temple treasure. The soldiers themselves told where they were bound for. They say nothing of the treasure being left high and dry—they speak only of its capture."

"That is all as it should be. Now we must send forward the letter signed with the seal of Pilate. In the morning it must go to the Temple. Then let the priests fall upon the Roman dogs!"

XVII

THE messenger bearing Pilate's flowery letter of thanks to Ben Rashid had delivered it as he had been commanded; "with all ceremony and pomp." The old Jew's soul was black within him as he read, but he bit his lips and held back his words. He would rather have eaten a boat-load of desert sand than swallow this bitter medicine. But he took it in silence.

He knew the ways of men. He did not blame the thieves, neither did he blame the watchmen for gathering up the silver and gold from the sand and abandoning their posts. But in his heart was deep bitterness against Pontius Pilate and he cursed the three flitty, white Greek girls. Even when they were his, he had had no pleasure of them and under his breath he called them "birdies." But he controlled himself in the presence of the courier. In fact, a little overreached himself to appear genial, for he ordered a costly silk robe to be taken from between the boards of his personal presses and presented to the Roman messenger.

But as soon as the man had gone, he ordered his fastest camels to be saddled and bridled and set off for Jerusalem, riding himself on the white one, the rare albino camel with pink eyes. She was the pride of the whole sand-sailing fleet, but her wind was short, and she really had all she could do to keep up with the others.

After travelling day and night Ben Rashid and his men reached the walls of Jerusalem several hours before dawn. He knew nothing of the stranded Temple treasure far in the wilderness north of the city and he knew nothing of the fast messenger Pilate had ordered to fly to Syria "by day and by night and not to tarry for much food or rest or sleep and not to be delayed by heat or wind or storm, but to press forward with his special order, and even to commandeer horses, camels, and anything necessary to speed them on." These were the very words. And, to make doubly sure, a second messenger, charged with the same message and armed with a like scroll of authority, followed five hours behind. Ben Rashid knew none of all these happenings.

The doors in the walls of Jerusalem were locked when they arrived, and, with all his hammering and calling out, Ben Rashid was unable to have them opened before the proper time. The party camped by the main gate waiting for sunrise, when the trumpets would sound. Then the heavy chains would clank as they fell from the hooks inside, and the sleepy watchmen, lazy and yawning, would slowly drag open the great doors.

When the doors finally opened Ben Rashid went straight to the Temple, for there he knew he would find Caiaphas, the high priest, at morning services. But already the streets had life. Roman sentinels were passing out of the city gates to patrol all the roads in the vicinity.

Sulla thundered by in a chariot drawn by four horses. Ever since his release from the dungeon and his sharp interview with Pilate he had been driving up and down, in one gate and out another, through one road and back another with his eyes pointed like needles, growling like a mad dog and snorting with wild hog-like noises at all he encountered. In his belt hung two swords as well as a large dagger, and on the floor of the chariot he had a stout rope. This time he would not be found unprepared. He wore a brass breast-plate studded with spikes, front and back, and instead of the plumes in his helmet, the top was mounted with the curved blade of a battle-axe. This time his enemies, once found, would not escape.

He gave no room to travellers on the road, and merchants with loaded asses had all they could do to get out of his way. He beat his horses with the short chariot whip not caring whether he struck with the lash or the wood of the handle. He bound the reins about his arms and thundered on and on. But nowhere could he find a trace of those for whom he searched.

Ben Rashid went straight into the inner court of the Temple. He unfolded his black and white prayer shawl and, placing it over his shoulders, took hold of the long silken fringe and joined the morning prayers. As soon as these were ended the priests with Caiaphas and Ben Rashid went into another hall.

"Peace be with you," Caiaphas greeted Rashid.

"With you peace," came the formal reply.

The moment these conventional bows were over they all began talking at once. "What is to be done!" "Who can lead us now!" "All is lost!" "Roman dogs, their very breath is corrupt!"

When the clamor abated somewhat, Caiaphas told Ben Rashid what was rumored around in the streets about the great tribute from the Jews in Rome to the Holy Temple.

"For some unknown reason the whole caravan has been stopped in the wilderness, and Pilate's soldiers have gone forward to take it. We saw them leave. They say they go to protect it only, but the silver and the gold we will never see. And our holy vestments and sacred relics he refuses. . . he refuses to give back to us. Ourselves we went into his riggish towers, into his unclean whorish den, and himself with his own foul mouth he refused. May darkness fall upon his days and fire upon his

240

nights, and may his soul be rent with fury and destruction!"

Ben Rashid listened. He did not show the letter he had received from Pilate thanking him for his present. This did not seem to be a proper time for such matters.

The high priest continued; "We must proclaim before all our people that the dark hour for lamentation has come. Our land is lost, our treasure robbed, the power of our court is reduced, our sacred robes and vessels, the holy part of our life and tradition, are taken away and we ourselves in body and soul have become the slaves of unclean beasts!"

"Wait! With haste nothing can be accomplished," reasoned another priest.

And a third said; "If we put on the clothes of mourning and sprinkle ashes on our heads our people will mourn with us and they will lack the spirit and temper necessary to drive out the Roman dogs."

"Yes." A fourth agreed; "Now is the time to tear them up by the roots and shake them in the wind."

"But will the people rise up against them?" asked Caiaphas doubtfully.

"We should wait a day or more. The streets are filling up with pilgrims and soon Jerusalem will be bursting with life."

"But the synagogues are against us," said Caiaphas. "People come now to worship in these hole-in-the-corner places. And no wonder! Why should they come to the Temple if they know that each bit of silver that they contribute is taken away by the Romans? And the vestments and holy vessels defiled by pagan hands."

Then another priest spoke and said; "There was also some resentment last year about the pigeons for sacrifice and also about the money-changers."

Caiaphas frowned. "These are trifles compared to the other outrages."

"We should wait another day," repeated the same priest.

"How many synagogues are there now in Jerusalem?" asked Ben Rashid.

"Near a hundred," said one.

"Let there be five hundred!" cried Caiaphas in anger. "What matter is it? The Temple is robbed of its treasure. Must we stand silent? The soldiers have gone into the desert. Now is the time to strike. Call the men and let them mount the walls and sound the trumpets. I will myself appear in the turret and proclaim the facts."

"Stay! Not so hasty. Let us strike with reason," said another.

And yet another added; "We must play to win, for if we lose, our lives are done."

While this highly treasonable talk was taking place in the Temple, and Caiaphas was urging instant action, Rongus was driving full speed from Bethlehem to the walls of Jerusalem.

That very morning, while Ben Rashid waited for the gates to open and Sulla with his chariot drawn by four fretted horses was dashing in and out, turning about madly and rushing on in any direction that offered—that very morning, Rongus put aside his golden breast-plate, and dressed himself in Sulla's toga. And he also put on Sulla's plumed helmet and the leather corslet, the one that was studded with brass nails, the same that they had taken away from him during that fast

243

ride when they went seeking justice at the point of a dagger and ended up at a village barber's!

Rongus drove the Roman bronze chariot. With one hand he held the reins and in the other he carried a small roll of parchment, the sheep-skin that had been shaven of all its contents except the seal and signature of Pontius Pilate, and reinscribed.

On the floor of the chariot, well under the bronze apron, and covered over with a sack cloth, was Barzor. Driving down the paved road in this fashion, Rongus saluted any Roman soldiers that they happened to pass. And the soldiers returned the salute respectfully.

"Go on Rongus," said Barzor from under the sack. "Ride straight into their teeth and stop for nothing."

The chariot went ahead full speed.

As they came to the gate of the city, Sulla with his four horses pounding madly, passed them and turned into the roadway leading round the outside of the wall. Sulla half lifted his arm in passing salutation but, suddenly, he caught himself. He looked hard. But already the other chariot was turning the corner and he lost sight of the face of the driver.

His eye, however, now fell on the leather corslet and he recognized it. And then the other things—all, all were his. Mingled rage and joyful anticipation almost stifled him.

"At last, great Jupiter!" he roared. "Aah!" And he jerked at the lines swinging the four horses round a sharp turn. The hoofs slipped on the pavement and a shower of sparks shot out beneath them. Again they were off.

"Destiny! Oh, Destiny! Bring us only to grips, oh Gods! Come on there!" he cried to his horses and cracked his whip.

Then he dashed through the gate after the other chariot but alas! . . . his enemy was blocked from his view by the bazaars and buildings.

He drove up the broadest street and cried; "Make way! In the name of Cæsar, make way!" And as he rushed along he glared in every direction for a glimpse of this maddening infernal riding chariot—his chariot, with the horses and sporting his helmet and toga!

Goshen College
Library

Now he howled and beat the horses so cruelly that they reared and almost threw him out.

In the meantime Rongus had reached the steps of the Temple.

"Lose no time!" ordered Barzor, crouched on the floor of the chariot.

"Here, you," called Rongus to one of the Temple bailiffs guarding the animals brought for sacrifice. "Here is a command from his excellency the Governor. Deliver it without delay!"

With these words he threw the small roll of parchment into the Temple court. The horses pranced with impatience and, without delay, he wheeled about and started back.

The roll was snatched up by the nearest bailiff and quickly handed to a half-priest in the court-yard. He took it to the entrance of the inner court and a rabbi brought it in haste to the high priests.

Caiaphas with trembling hand unrolled the parchment. But his eyes grew dim and he gave the document over to one of the younger priests saying; "Now it is the end. The first words are enough.

246

The world becomes black before my eyes. Read!
Read while the walls and everything that you hold
sacred spin before your eyes. Now is our voice
strangled and our power slain."

The priest read; "What you might have given
cheerfully, you refused to surrender. And now
even the security that you might have had—even
that will be taken away from you. The treasure
from Rome will also be used to bring water into
Jerusalem. . . ."

From all sides rose a stifled murmur.

The priest continued the reading; "All consid-
eration for your customs and beliefs has been
generously allowed but in one point you are now
required to yield. It is ordered from this day that
Roman money stamped with the seal of our em-
pire and the head of Tiberius Caesar shall be, and
must be, accepted as proper currency throughout
the land of Judea, in every city and village, and
even within the innermost confines of the Temple.
(Signed) Pontius Pilate."

"Sound the horns!" cried Caiaphas. "Call the
multitude together!"

"The horns! The horns!" called another.

"Prepare for a state of siege. This will be our darkest Passover."

"It is Pilate's signature and imprint with his own seal," said Ben Rashid. "I know it well."

"Every Roman insult has opened a wound—and every wound is a Hebrew grave! Now the earth falls over us!"

"The horns! Let them sound clear and without delay. Blow you trumpets! Rend the air with your blast and call together our people!"

"To the walls!"

Caiaphas beat his breast.

XVIII

THE moment Rongus turned his chariot in its course, Sulla caught sight of it. He let out a wild cry of joy.

Barzor, crouched on the floor and hearing the pounding noise of the four-horsed chariot in pursuit, looked out from under the covering.

"It's the Roman captain!" he called. "Better make speed. The same road back. Stop for nothing!"

Rongus threw loose the reins and the chariot shot forward as though sprung from a giant crossbow. Now they rode a deadly race.

In another moment they were past the city

gate. The shadow of the wall crossed their faces like a monster's blink.

Free of streets and crowds, the road lay broad and clear before them. The pavement swept beneath and like a thunder-roll with its echo behind, they tore through.

"By Hercules! He is mine! Oh!" Sulla beat with his whip and each blow was a splitting crack. "Oh! He is mine! Faster."

There was a distance of about ten lengths between them. But Rongus held his lead and kept the crown of the road. His face was hardened with resolution. His chariot contained another rider, it was heavier, and he had but two horses against the Roman's four. But he held the center of the road and he kept his lead.

Now Barzor suddenly threw off the sack that covered him and Sulla saw both of them before him.

"Both of them!" he cried. "The gods are good at last. Both are mine! Oh! Faster! On!" He whirled his lash with the joy of expectation.

"One league done," called Barzor, crouching low to give balance to the flying cart. "Keep on

Rongus. One more league and then let him win his grave. Don't slacken. Give line and let them run."

Now for the first time Rongus laid the whip across the horses' flanks. They plunged ahead, tugging with all the strength and fury that was in them. Their bright blood was stirred up near to boiling.

The race was on.

They dashed along with a plunging rumble and maddening rattle. And still Rongus kept ahead.

The Roman swayed uneasily, first trying the right side of the road and then cutting into the left. But he only held his ground and beat his horses with fury.

"Half a league more!" called Barzor. "Only as far as the cisterns. And when you are near these wells let him draw up alongside. . . . Then, Rongus, you may try your strength. Half a league more!"

"We could run him dry!"

"No. We must stop him at the wells. Give him room and let him try to twist off our wheel . . . and when he is close. . . ."

"I understand!" called Rongus.

251

They ran.

The road cleared itself before them and the dust they raised blinded all behind. On they went but now the Roman was closing in and gaining ground.

"Let him come on the right side," said Barzor. "But watch our wheel."

Not far off were the cisterns and they could see the women carrying their clay jugs of water.

Sulla was pushing forward. His red face shone with excitement. Only violence and destruction could satisfy his deadly lust.

Now the Roman came alongside and tugged on the left line to swing the horses in and cut off the others. But Rongus kept an even speed and would not give up what road they needed. At the same time Rongus caused the chariot to sway a bit, first to the right and then to the left. This was just what the Roman wanted. Here was his chance to cut in with his wheel and shear off their wheel.

They drove on, the mad pace unslackened.

Now they were side by side. Sulla fixed his gaze on the wheel just ahead of his. They almost rubbed. He drew in closer and hung over the side to watch for the instant when he could wedge his wheel between. They ran dangerously close together.

Then the angle opened and now was his chance. He lashed blindly with his whip.

"Now!" called Barzor.

The two chariots were abreast. Suddenly Rongus swung out his arm and lifted the Roman out of his chariot. He held him aloft and drew in his lines with the other arm.

The four horses and empty chariot shot ahead and Sulla hanging in the air waved his arms and legs frantically. His surprise was so great that he had no wind in him to cry out, and only a stifled gasp escaped.

The pace broke. The wells were near. The women around, seeing the commotion, took up their buckets and jars of water and ran to a safe distance.

The driverless chariot came to a halt and so too did Rongus, still holding aloft the struggling Roman in his iron grip.

Then he threw him down upon the ground. But as soon as Sulla could recover his feet he drew his broad sword and cried out; "Man or demon! Stand, ho!" He threw himself forward.

Rongus stepped down from the chariot and watching him with a cool eye, seized hold of his arm and bore down upon it until the sword fell from the Roman's grip. He bent him double and he did not release his hold until he had drawn from the Roman's belt the second sword and the dagger. When these were thrown to the ground he pushed the Roman back with such violence that he whirled his arms in the air a dozen times to recover his balance.

Once more the furious Sulla pitched forward. This time he bent low and charged with his cleaver helmet. But Rongus stepped quickly aside and the Roman ran himself to the ground.

Now he threw off his helmet and with bare fists shot out blindly for one more desperate encounter. And this was his last, for Rongus lifted him clear off the ground and again held him high in the air.

"Hgg, hgg!" the water in the Roman's throat gurgled.

"Into the well!" cried Barzor.

Rongus moved a step or two forward and threw the struggling Roman down into the broad cistern.

The women seeing this from a short distance away screamed. Then Rongus and Barzor stepped into their chariot and drove the horses forward.

Rongus said; "It seemed a shallow well and he may try to follow us."

"Don't fear," Barzor replied. "I have cut his chariot's traces. But anyway we have no time to lose."

They started off and at a lively pace they drove on towards Bethlehem.

Fortunately for Sulla the cistern was not high, neither was the water much over his belt. The women came back and looked over the top and laughed at him.

One old crone even said; "Now isn't it a foolish thing to get down there? What did you want in there anyway?"

Another said; "They have no clean wells in Jerusalem and now they come here to spoil ours also."

Then they got the rope that was in the bottom of his chariot. It took eight women and girls to drag him out.

The old women among them said; "Such a leaden and beslubbered lump I never saw in all my long years."

XIX

In the meantime before the horns sounded from the Temple turrets the three Greek girls in the Towers had been enjoying themselves.

Earlier in the week workmen had been called in to make a new floor in their quarters. The three carved malachite columns were brought to Jerusalem and broken up into small pebbles and made smooth on one surface. Now came the task of setting them into the wet cement spread over the floor. But the girls were tormentors and did not let the apron-men do their task.

First they came from the bath in their bright red gowns and said; "May we walk here? And over there? And in that room? In this place too? And anywhere?"

"Is it still wet?" asked another.

The third said; "How long does it take to dry?"

"Oh, it's long," said the first. "And my hair dries in only a little over an hour."

"A slow-sanded hour," corrected the second, meaning that some hour-glasses were fast and some slower.

When Zozo heard them talking to the workmen he came in and sent them away for they had no right to speak to strange men.

But when he was not looking they came forward all three together and began their skittish prattle. "May we walk here too?"

They stole pebbles out of the soft floor and concealed them in their hands and then they were good—very good. They stood at the far end and looked on quietly. Then they decided to give back the little stones to the workmen and they called them forward and the eldest gave hers first.

When the men went back to work the second said; "But you have not taken mine? Here are more." She held out her hand.

Under his breath the foreman said; "A pair of these flit-gills would drive a man crazy."

Then after a time up piped the third; "I have stones too. Why don't you take mine also?"

The foreman added; "But three of them together could give a bronze statue the jumping itch!"

Now Buncha, the Babylonian dwarf, waddled into the hall and sent them along.

"Out with you. Skip, ho! And your hands, look at them. Dirty! Shame. Go back to the fountain. Wash a dog in the seven seas and in a moment he is again full of mud."

She led them to the fountain and saw that every hand was properly washed.

Then the girls spied Pilate eating his breakfast and before the dwarf could stop them they ran forward with careless abandon and their gowns flew open.

"Do-do," they called. "We have such a good idea."

"Well what is it?" Pilate asked, still not fully awake from his troubled sleep.

"Well Do-do. You must say 'yes' and then we will tell you."

"No. That I will not and cannot do."

"Oh, Do-do. How disagreeable you are today. That is not nice. And we thought you were so nice." These words were said by the youngest and she moved close to him.

"Now run along and play and leave your Do-do alone."

"But you do not know our idea."

"We all thought of it at the same time and that is why it is surely good."

"Well—What is it?"

"Oh, it would be so nice."

"We would just love it," said the second.

"And you would like it too," added the third.

"But what is it?"

"We would like . . . Take us on a boat ride."

"A boat ride. It would be heavenly. Just ourselves and nobody else."

"Yes. We love the rocking and the ups and downs."

"Well I declare!" said Pilate. "Here we are encircled by leagues and leagues of sand and they want a boat ride! Put a log in the pool and sit on it!"

"You know Do-do. When we get into the pool, the other women run out. They do not like us. But then we laugh at them and talk in Greek which they cannot understand."

"And Do-do," said another. "Tell them not to be looking at us through the cracks."

"I will stuff them full of pepper and when I know they are looking, I will blow it into their eyes. Truly I will. And you know why? Well, because . . ."

"Oh, Do-do. Be nice. Take us for a boat ride."

Then Buncha came into the hall and drove them away. "Out of here! What, ho! And away. You kettle of flopping fish. Skip."

And the girls ran back to their rooms much pleased with their mischief for they knew very well that they had no right to interrupt their Do-do when he was at his breakfast. This was the time when the secretaries reported to him and received their orders for the day.

Buncha called out to Zozo; "You black son of bile, can't you keep them in their rooms?" And she shook her large wooden key with the metal teeth threateningly.

"She will be the death of me yet!" Zozo said. "The frog is ever at me."

And it was then that they heard the trumpets sound from the walls of the Temple.

Buncha ran to the terrace and looked over. Then she came back with the exciting news.

"The priests are mounting the walls. They are signalling the horns to sound again. The streets are filling up. The crowds are moving toward the Temple. There they blow again. Something is up. Perhaps they have heard about the treasure. Perhaps they think the soldiers have gone forward to capture it instead of rescuing it for them. They are suspicious and the word treason slides lightly on their wet lips. There are the horns again."

"Go Buncha and look once more."

The dwarf ran again to the balcony and in another moment she returned. "The seven high priests stand on the wall and seem waiting for the people to assemble. They are waving their arms and calling them closer as though they mean to address them."

261

"Send for our captains!"

Only four captains appeared.

"Where are the rest!" Pilate shouted.

"They are on duty. Some have gone forward with the troops into the desert and the others are out with their men on the roads about. . . . The guards watching for the Arab and the Jew. Two are in the Gethsemane grove."

"Have you horses? And how many charioteers?"

"Six units of ten."

"Send out all sixty chariots. Let them trot through the streets from one end to the other. And wherever the fusty plebeians are gathered run by— divide the rabble up and then turn about and scatter them wide. Keep all sixty running up and down. Go! And let them start without delay."

Buncha approved of this measure.

Then Pilate turned to his secretaries and said; "Request in writing that the priests appear before me. And see that this is delivered instantly."

XX

BUT the priests sent back word that they would not come.

"Then if they will not come to me," said Pilate, "I will go to them."

"Not now! Not now!" said Buncha. "The chariots have begun clearing the streets. The rumble and clatter prevent the priests from addressing the noisy rabble. Some are throwing stones at the charioteers."

"I will put stones down their throats!"

"Stay here until it quiets down."

"Call the bowmen. Let them take up their positions on the city walls and here in the Tower. Have them mount their cross-bows on stands and set up the stone-hurling catapults in each tower. Call back the soldiers from the roads and let them mount the walls and stand in readiness. What are an Arab and a Jew compared to a whole country! If we cannot take those two then I will proclaim them free and make them officers if they will come forward. I swear it! And I will do it. If not today I will do it tomorrow or Friday. By the stars in heaven I will do it. How long must I wait?"

"Patience, Excellency. It will all turn for the best." Buncha tried to pacify the troubled man. "Soon the army from Syria will arrive. From Damascus they come hard as iron. And down the valley through Galilee; they are no soft-beaked fledglings or nest cuddlers. And how they can ride. Ah! they are like those from my own land. No corky ones there."

"I will go to the priests."

"No, let them come here."

"They refuse!"

"Then wait. They must come. Today is Wednesday, tomorrow Thursday and Friday at sundown begins the Passover. Sometime between now and then they will need their vestments and the golden breast-plate, the one that is set with twelve jewels. How will they get them? They must come!"

"They may send servants."

"You need not entrust servants with their holy vestments. Let them come themselves. This is only a spit in the fire. They will cool off."

The sixty chariots trotted through the streets and some of them kept going round and round the Temple walls. The startled populace scuttled here and there before them. The rumble of the wheels on the rough pavement could be heard even outside the city gates.

The priests stood stricken, for against this they were powerless. But anger lit their faces, and they paced the Temple walls and raised their arms on high.

Only when the noonday sun was above them did they give up and descend from the high walls of the Temple to take fresh counsel. But the chariots continued their rounds, in and out, here and there, some coming and others going.

By this time also the swing-about stone-throwing engines were mounted on the city towers and heavy steel cross-bows with arrows in their slots were beside them.

Sulla trailed back into Jerusalem, a sorry sight. The traces of his chariot were crudely tied together and, followed by the jeers of his comrades, he made his way to the barracks. Here he had no word to utter; he could only grunt.

He hid himself in the stable with the horses and rolled into a bin of straw. But the others knew just where he was and they said among themselves that the gods had granted him the favor he had begged and that he had "come to grips" with the infernal two. In fact they were certain of it.

Later in the day one of the captains went down and called out; "Sulla! Where are you? We have good news. The soldiers have discovered their house. . . . Here, come out!"

He crawled forward on all fours. "Where! Where! Where!" he gasped.

"In Bethlehem; and there is a yard in front with a stone wall. The place is marked and it will be watched. But the gate is strong."

"How strong can a gate be!" Sulla bellowed.

"We can break it through."

But now Sulla was on his feet.

"No you won't! No! They are mine. By all the gods they belong to me!"

With these words he staggered out and up the steps and over the arch into the Towers.

Once more he appeared before Pilate.

"They are in Bethlehem!" he cried. "And now we can take them. We know the house. Myself I saw them today!"

"You saw them!"

"Yes. We ran together for a space and I beat them out. And then we came to grips and. . . . And I lost them."

"Ha, ha! Oh you soft butter! Your hands were upon them and you lost them. What are you? A slippery jelly! Get out!"

"We fought in earnest, I say! But they escaped me."

"What is it you are made of? Your bone, your muscle, your blood, your brain—all is mixed as in a soup. Oh! what a hotchpotch you are! Get out, I say!"

"But now we have them. They are behind a garden wall in Bethlehem. Let me take a battering ram and ten of the shockers, and every wall and house in Bethlehem will be leveled down to the ground. Even if they were built of granite and iron we will powder it, and I will bring them before you. I swear it!"

"Take the ram. Take the men. But go! Go! Out of my sight you flap-mouthed fool. Go!"

With ten heavy men of the artillery Sulla mounted a battering-ram on a pair of chariot wheels and started off for Bethlehem, cheered by the guards behind him. The ram was one of the lighter ones and consisted of a log to which were attached iron rings that served as handles. At one end was a bronze ram's head with long curved horns. This was the battling end of the log.

Soon after they passed through the gate of the city the evening trumpets sounded. Then the great rotten timbered doors of Jerusalem swung slowly together and, with a rattling of chains, they were locked for the night.

In the city streets all seemed quiet, but behind the walls and within the houses there was much agitation.

XXI

AFTER the encounter with Sulla, Barzor and Rongus had hurried on to Bethlehem. There was no time to lose.

Yaba was in the yard loading the two camels with various boxes and things belonging to them.

"We cannot remain here much longer," said the gray-headed Arab.

Barzor did not seem surprised. He only asked; "Will you take the asses also?"

"No. They are poky. I mean to leave them here."

"Good. And the salt?" asked Barzor.

"We can buy the bags in the next village. I shall

get four large sacks. Everything is in order and our men are chafing with impatience."

Rongus interrupted him; "Where is Mariamne and where is the blind David?"

"I sent them away!" said Yaba.

"Away!"

"Yes. They should not remain here. The Romans are certain to be upon us at any moment."

"But where did they go?"

"The girl said you would know where to find her."

"On the steps of . . ."

"Yes. Let us hurry."

Then Barzor said to Rongus; "Don't fret. Come along. Tomorrow you will be free and can go where you will. I promise."

They ran into the house and gathered up a few things. Rongus found a wax tablet on his bed and the following words were scratched upon it by Mariamne; "At the steps of the Temple."

He read these words over and over, while Barzor drew out from its secret hiding place the ancient crown of the Jews, that odd band of gold that had been sealed in Herod's tomb.

For a moment he held the crown in his hands, as though he were about to place it on his own head, and his lips whispered; "I am roguery—king of the world." But then he suddenly cried out against himself; "No, no, no! This is a madness that springs from life itself. It is right. It is just." And he quickly wrapped the crown in a silken cloth and tucked it away in his bosom.

Once more Rongus threw aside the Roman toga and corslet, and once more strapped on his cherished golden breast-plate Over this he put back his Arab garments, closing them up so as to hide the golden armor completely.

In a moment they were back into the yard. Yaba was now tying up the three asses, while his black slave held the camel ropes.

"I am sending the black along with the camels," said Yaba. "And, after you leave, I will bolt the gates from within and climb over the wall."

"We are ready," Barzor announced.

Yaba signaled to his slave who went forward leading both camels out of the yard.

Rongus stepped into the waiting chariot but before mounting beside him, Barzor turned to

Yaba; "In all things you deserve praise. All was faithfully and skilfully done. When we next meet we shall be in the field and the open land that we know so well. Tell the men that victory is ours." Rongus cracked his whip and they were off.

There were still several hours of daylight and to ride out openly in a Roman chariot while dressed in Arab robes was an act of courageous defiance. Roman spear-men or foot-guards however would not be able to stop them and they left the road as soon as they had passed the city gate and cut across the hard desert sand avoiding the soft wave-like billows as well as the thorny and rocky places.

Their progress was not fast and now and then they halted to view the surrounding country. From a high spot they saw the roads in the distance filled with pilgrims and travellers, all going to Jerusalem for the holy services. Some carried their own provisions in large sacks and others led beasts of burden heavily laden, with utensils dangling from cords that tied the packs. Here and there, a line of smoke from a village baker's busy oven mounted high into the air. Every house was being cleaned from one end to another. The benches and tables

272

were in the open being scrubbed with hemp dipped in sand and water. Metal pots were being purified over the burning embers and they could hear the tapping of the little mallets that were packing down the fresh clay to make clean floors in the huts

They drove on.

"We are going to Jerusalem again?" said Rongus joyfully, catching sight of the walls in the distance.

"No, Rongus. We will drive a bit to the east but we shall not be far from Jerusalem."

They passed the city of Netophah and went on slowly to Bethany. Now they were but a league and a half from the Holy City and it was necessary to proceed with much caution.

At this distance they could see the spear-men pacing along the top of the walls of Jerusalem. And they could also see against the setting sun the mounted cross-bows and the stone-hurlers in the turrets.

Twilight came upon them quickly and now they could go ahead with greater freedom. Rounding the fertile valley just east of the Mount of Olives their view of Jerusalem was cut off and they came to the gardens and home of Rabbi Ezra, son of Joshua.

As they drove in, the servants ran forward and took the horses and chariot to the shed behind the house.

"I bring a Hebrew with me," Barzor announced, entering the house with Rongus.

But the room was filled with many people and candles were burning along each wall. For alas! the magnificent Rabbi Ezra, the beloved son of the great teacher, Joshua, was dying. He was propped up with large cushions and he smiled when he saw Barzor enter.

"But what is this?" said Barzor.

Some put their fingers to their lips and others merely pointed to the chair in which the enfeebled rabbi was resting.

"But only a month ago when I was here last. . . ."

"A month ago," smiled the dying rabbi, "was a different moon, and a different sky, and the sea was also less stirred up, and everything was different except the good Lord in Heaven. Oh my son, my son."

"But everything is ready and I have brought . . ."

274

He did not finish what he began saying but took from his bosom the crown and, without unwrapping it, placed it in the old man's trembling hands.

"My son, oh, my son," these were the only words he could say but his emotion was great and tears came to his eyes. "The whole land should give you blessing, my son."

"But now Rabbi—What now?"

The old man was silent.

"But, Rabbi. Here everything is arranged and ready. Here is the crown. The Romans are ready to strike and the black Temple priests are prepared to throw themselves headlong upon them. Now is our time. Each is weakened by the other and now you are to step in and call together the elders of the synagogues and appoint your own king. And the Romans and the Herods would flee or remain to die. I have done all possible from our side. Further I cannot go. Oh, Rabbi Ezra, what is to be done?"

"Man arranges and God disarranges. But His wisdom is great. He saw that I was already old. But everything will be accomplished with His will. There are younger hearts and braver souls. And

275

what you have already done will be taken forward by my three sons. They are now in Jerusalem and are meeting with the loyal elders. But there is one thing we cannot understand. News has come to us about the Temple tribute. Has it been stolen?"

"No. It is as safe as though it were already here. This was the only way I knew to get the whole legion out of Jerusalem. Without troops, Pilate is helpless."

"But the chariots have been coursing the streets all day long and the people have been unable to gather in any one place."

"In the morning if they go forth again we will draw them on. My young companion Rongus can outride any of them. And I promise you that by evening there will be very few chariots left in Jerusalem. Then let Caiaphas sound his horns and let all tumble together. In the meantime the hundred synagogues of Jerusalem will enlighten their people and after the Temple has driven out the Romans, you. . . . Oh, Ezra, I planned it for you. But now it will be your sons. They will lead against the black cousins of Herod in the Temple and against the false king Antipas."

"The young men understand and are ready to give their lives for the liberation of their people."

"And my own men in the desert are waiting and we come close tomorrow night and stand ready.

"Tomorrow night is already Thursday and all must be accomplished before the Sabbath candles are lit on Friday evening. Oh, my son! So much you have done. So much."

"What I have done, I have done. Long before the black rule of Herod my people were princes and your family were the rightful lords of the Temple. You have been driven like an outcast and are forbidden to enter the Holy City and I. . . . Well, you know what I have become. The world holds little in store for either of us if our lives cannot be given for our own people. You for yours, and I for mine. If together we can throw off this yoke, then the Jews and the Arabs will live in peace for evermore, and your eldest will be king of the Jews and none other will dare claim to stand in his place."

"Well spoken, Barzor," said the feeble rabbi and he kissed the crown in his hands. "Forever in peace, but if we fail," and he held his finger up in warning. "If we fail, then there will never be peace between my people and your people. Because unhappiness is restless and thirsts for adventure and adventure must lead to quarrel. And our roots will hang forever in the air."

Then Rongus came forward and kneeled down before old Ezra; "Bless me Rabbi, for tomorrow I will be free."

"I bless you, son. I bless you tonight and I bless you also in your freedom. Let there be happiness. But never great riches. For there is trouble in the gain of wealth, perplexity in the full tide of its abundance and pain in its loss. Seek happiness alone and you will live."

"I will be happy. I will. I will."

XXII

Not until it was quite dark did Sulla arrive at Bethlehem with the ten shockers and the smashing battering-ram. But, fearing some trick, they approached the house with great caution. Soon they grew bolder. Then they woke up the whole neighborhood with their shouts and the lights from their burning torches.

The heavy bronze-tipped log was untied from its wheels and dragged into position. Soon they lifted it and began swinging it back and forth with increasing motion. Then they came closer and each blow gave a pounding crash to the gate.

Some of the dried clay, loosed by these terrific

shocks, fell down upon them from the top of the wall. But they pounded on. And Sulla cried out; "By Hercules let it smash! Hold ready your shields and swords! When the doors are down, in we rush!"

The gate could not stand many blows and soon it collapsed. The soldiers now seized their torches and with swords drawn rushed into the yard. But, alas! There was nothing there except the three asses tied to the wall. And these lazy beasts were so unconcerned that they did not even turn their heads to see what was going on.

In the house nothing was found except the wax tablet with some words scratched upon it. Sulla took it up and read the message that Mariamne had written to Rongus. He took the tablet with him and because of his disappointment and because of his anger, he kicked the asses as he went through the yard.

It was now quite late and the soldiers had a weary march back to Jerusalem wheeling the great log after them. When they reached the walls of the city they stretched out in the grass and went to sleep for the remainder of the night, until the gates should open again at sunrise.

TWO THIEVES

At the same time the old Arab Yaba with the two laden camels and his slave were cutting across a wide arc of land west and north of Jerusalem. On their way, by the light of the faint moon, they gathered loose branches and knots of thorn-wood and when they came to a high place they built a small fire. When the fire was burning brightly they threw on three great handfuls of salt and the flames flared up with a brilliant yellow blaze.

Before dawn came upon them they were far out into the wilderness and seven signal fires had been kindled and flared three times when the salt was showered upon them. At dawn they found a rocky ravine and here they refreshed themselves with food and sleep.

In the Towers beside the barracks in Jerusalem, Buncha, the Babylonian dwarf, left her bed a dozen times during the night to walk up and down the halls in her thick white woolen night-gown fringed with deep borders of purple. She looked into the various rooms, with candle in hand, and she paced up and down the corridors, and she went out on the balconies to look at the stars. But she also threw her watchful eye along the city walls and caught

281

the glint of the watchman's spear in this place and in that. She knew where they were supposed to stand and what distance along the wall each was required to pace.

Then she saw the engines of war. The jagged shadow in the dark was the giant steel cross-bow and she saw also the stone-throwing catapults set in the corner towers and the tripod mounted vats that had great ladles for pouring down flaming oil from the tops of the walls. And here and there she saw the pyramids of small stones ready for the hand-slingers.

She saw everything. Nothing seemed to escape her searching eye. She saw the signal fire when it appeared on a distant hill and she watched it closely. In about an hour she saw another, and again a third a long, long distance away.

Then she went inside the Towers and paced up and down the long halls, fretful and with short nervous steps. Finally she came to Pilate's private chamber and, with candle before her, whispered through the heavy curtain; "Are you asleep, Excellency?"

"No, Buncha. I am trouble-tossed."

She lifted the curtain and came forward.

"All is well, there is nothing to fear."

She put the candle down and sat on the edge of his couch.

"I am quite awake, you may tell me everything."

"There is nothing to say. All is well. The guards are upon the walls and their steel flashes in the light of the moon."

"And the stars—what do they say?"

"They are dim tonight and the overcast clouds are moving fast across the sky."

"What does that tell?"

"Anything or nothing. As the wind goes so the feather blows. And it all means nothing."

"Then are we safe?"

"Yes. All is well. But tell me, Excellency, how far in the desert was the Temple tribute?"

"Three days . . . Perhaps only two."

"Two there and two back that makes four. Then the legion will be back."

"Yes."

"And tell me also. . . . How far is Syria?

"Oh, far, too far."

"But I must know."

"Days and nights."

"How many?"

"Above Judea is Samaria, that is two days but a runner may reach it in one. And then above Samaria is Galilee and that is another two but a fast messenger can cross it in one. Above Galilee is Syria but the main legion may be in Damascus and because of the hills and rivers, that is another two days."

"But there has been trouble in Galilee and the army may be standing on the borderland."

"Even then they could not be here before the start of the Jewish holy days."

The dwarf walked up and down and to cover her nervousness she said; "Why should they come from Syria anyway? All is well. We do not need them. The Jews are proud and arrogant and no army can humble them. But why should we humble them? First they split hairs with each other, then they flame up with a violent anger."

"True Buncha. I would rather play with serpents than meddle with the Temple priests. But the vestments must stay here until they actually require them."

"Yes. We are strong only if we remain unmoved. And justice is on the side of strength."

"Can we hold a solid front?"

"Today and tomorrow are our weakest hours. If we can hold over these days then all is well. Let the chariots be ready again and let them ride and divide the rabble. Bring more stones upon the walls, and more oil and arrows. Show all the strength that remains and they will think there is more concealed."

"Oh, Buncha! I am so weary of it all. And I long for home and Rome."

"Rome is exile in defeat and it is home only in victory. We must hold out!"

"True, Buncha. True." And he closed his weary eyes as the Babylonian dwarf took her tall candle and left the chamber.

XXIII

THE struggle began before noon and continued through the heat of the day. The disaster was complete.

It began near the walls of Jerusalem. Suddenly the guards on top of the walls spied Barzor and Rongus driving about in the bronze chariot dressed in their flowing Arab robes.

They raised the cry. Captains in their plumed helmets mounted the walls to make certain of the report.

"It's the Arab and the Jew!" they cried. "Out after them you! Out!"

At first only six or seven chariots started off in

pursuit but soon others came forth from opposite gates with the intention of heading off the hunted chariot.

Some soldiers rushed into the yard and set up the cry, and Buncha came to the balcony in the Towers to learn the cause of the commotion.

"Hold them here!" she cried, running back to Pilate. "Hold them!"

He sent for the captains, but it was too late, for Sulla himself now had the news and started off after them leading over thirty chariots through the northern gate.

"Hold them back!" ordered Pilate.

The captains ran to the bridge that arched across from the Towers to barrack walls, but they were too late.

"Send horses with riders after them and bring them back!"

The horses were saddled in haste and light riders dashed out through the streets, and out into the open desert.

But the chariots were now some distance off and coming together from different roads into a single direction. Some were even cutting across the hard desert ground to meet with their comrades. The riders on horseback did not see them and went on in wrong directions.

Barzor and Rongus with horses fresh were far ahead. Rongus held the reins lightly and gave his horses free play. He smiled. Now and then he tapped his breast with his free hand and felt his proud golden breast-plate beneath.

They ran north and west until they reached the main road to Joppa. And here the race began in earnest. But Barzor was holding back and calling to Rongus; "Easy, easy! Not too fast. Spare your horses, Rongus."

After they had gone ahead for a good hour with the Romans all in hot pursuit they came to a rocky pass in the hills and here by a stroke of good fortune were several merchants with a dozen or more asses laden with bales and bags of produce. The chariot slowed down and, halting for a moment, Barzor ran out into the road and cut the cords holding the packs. The bales and bags were scattered from one end of the road to another. The merchants shouted and cursed. But in another moment Barzor and Rongus were off.

This obstacle only delayed the Romans for a few minutes. They plowed their way through and the road now leading down hill gave them greater speed.

On and on they went. The country about them grew wild, rude and strange. When Barzor and Rongus looked back at their pursuers they saw that Sulla, himself driving the team of four, was leading the Romans. But their horses, due to the great activity of the day before, were in poor condition and a string of laggers now fell behind.

Now they broke into a trot, and great clouds of vapor came out of the horses' red nostrils. They were nearing the end and the place into which Barzor wanted to lead them was not far off.

He seemed to know every inch of the ground and when they passed a certain spot, Barzor took the reins from Rongus and drove ahead. Suddenly he turned off the road and ran over the hard sand. They bounced over the uneven ground.

As soon as the Romans behind them saw what had happened they too turned sharply off the road and cut across to shorten the distance.

They rattled over the uneven ground for a

few minutes then suddenly they struck into a great stretch of soft sand and all tumbled together.

The horses sank deeply and the wheels went down to their very hubs. Some of the chariots turned over and others stopped by the sudden impact broke their shafts and tore loose their traces.

The Romans called out wild cries and many behind them coming full speed into this soft ridge of moving sand were unable to halt suddenly and flung themselves upon the wreck. Some drew up in time. Those who had lagged behind now halted while the soldiers ran to the assistance of their comrades.

But there was nothing to be done. They loosened the traces and tried to save the horses. Some had sunk up to their bellies and were unable to move their legs. Some they pulled out by sheer force and others they rescued only to discover that the poor beasts had broken a limb and without delay they drew their daggers and slew them. Two had been gored by the broken shafts. Many others were bleeding from wounds.

The chariots too were dragged out but only half of them could travel on. Axles were broken or bent and many shafts and wheels were left lying in the soft sand.

Sulla alone cried out against everyone and wanted to go forward with what remained but the evil-doers were now far away and out of sight and his companions held him back. His own chariot was so buried in the sand that it had to be abandoned.

And slowly, painfully the sorry remains of this expedition with horses injured and chariots wrecked returned to Jerusalem at sundown.

XXIV

"Now you are free," said Barzor. "Here is the ring from my finger so that none will deny it. If you go into the desert show the ring and the Arabs will be your brothers. But if you go back to Jerusalem make certain first that the sons of Rabbi Ezra have come into power, otherwise your life will be in danger. Keep clear of Romans and do not go near to the Holy City for several days. We must neither of us be seen."

"I shall do as you say."

They unharnessed the horses, tied on two pads to serve as saddles, and mounted.

"But be careful, Rongus. You are too simple

for Roman tricks and without me you must be on your guard. And I, without you, will be lonesome. You have served faithfully and well and there is nothing that I can give you that would be a just reward."

"My freedom is enough, master," said Rongus. "And once I have found her, I shall come to you again."

"Yes, we shall see each other. . . . Even if you were my own son I could feel no deeper, and your freedom is a small token of my affection. Soon I hope, for, once the Romans and the priests are gone, we Arabs will often be seen in these parts. Goodbye Rongus, and may good-fortune follow you."

They embraced.

They left the chariot beside the road, and each went his own way.

Several times Rongus turned and waved still another farewell to his former master. But he had not gone more than several hundred paces when he felt alone and almost afraid. The impulse in him grew stronger and stronger to turn about and join Barzor again. He could not bear to leave him and feared for his own safety, but the clear oval face of Mariamne was mirrored in his mind and he went on and on aimlessly and in no definite direction. There was still an hour or more left before sundown.

From the top of a slight elevation he paused and looked back to catch a final glimpse of the Arab riding alone, a tiny spot in a vast vacant land. "Ah," he said to himself, "that is a man."

. . . .

The same loose sand that brought ruin to the Cæsars and the Herods was now to shift from under that structure built by the man who pitted himself against Rome. The temple of cunning and daring was tottering. Now the cracks were to open wide and columns and all were weakened and stood ready to fall.

First, the two runners sent to pursue the chariots and call them back had started off without seeing exactly the direction taken. They continued blindly and stupidly on the wrong road and went far north of the city instead of going westward.

But their orders were so emphatic that they dared not stop. They rode like mad and finding no chariots rode on and on until suddenly late in the afternoon they saw the marching troops bringing back the temple treasure. They spoke with the Roman captains and explained to them how they came upon this road. But the captains ordered them back at once and sent with them a message to Pilate.

Their horses were almost dead when they returned, for they forced them to run on and on for fear that the city gates would close with the lowering sun and lock them out.

Buncha read the message; "Announce to all that the treasure is safe and will be in the Holy City at dawn."

"Send out the criers!" called Pilate, "and let them call out from the gates and from the walls that the treasure is safe!"

And now the cracks of the structure built of cunning opened up wider and wider and the great columns began to tremble.

A messenger came from a certain house that stood outside the walls of the city on the slope of the Mount of Olives, near the grove of Gethsemane, and sought out the three sons to tell them that their beloved father the learned Rabbi Ezra, son of Joshua, was dead. This message was delivered secretly, and the young men started home at once. But as they passed through the crowded streets they heard the criers sing out the news of the treasure. A sudden burst of great joy come over the people.

Some cried; "Rejoice, rejoice, the treasure has been saved. The tribute from Rome is also a tribute from Jehovah. We are saved. The Lord is watching over his people."

And the eldest son said to the others as they walked in haste; "This is no time to lay claim to the kingdom of the Jews. There is mockery in the air."

And the youngest son added; "And that mountain preacher is again in the vicinity. And his followers are with him."

Then the other son spoke; "Our beloved father is dead. The Lord Jehovah has spared him the news of our failure. May his name be whispered in reverence forever and ever, until the end of time."

Not long upon the heels of the racing messengers, with the news of the treasure, returned the miserable remains of the great fleet of chariots.

"Look," called Buncha, who had been watching sharply from the balcony. "See what a wretched thing is crawling back to us."

Pilate had one glance. Then he breathed deeply and said; "If one Arab and one Jew together can accomplish all this, then it is well that we keep the Arabs far in the desert and the Jews right here under our nose. If two can do all this, then four of such would surely ruin us completely."

He was composed. The good news of the treasure tempered his humor.

Ben Rashid, after consulting with Caiaphas and the other Temple priests, went to the Towers and bowed low before Pilate.

"The people are rejoicing," he said. "But we are afraid that this is only a trick."

"Jew! Accuse me of no tricks!" cried Pilate.

"But here is your message and now your criers sing a different tune."

He unrolled the parchment and held it before him.

Pilate snatched it from his hand. His forehead reddened. "It's a forgery!" he cried. And he tore the command in twain. "It is vile. Base. Written by a demon and sealed with my seal and signed by my hand but not by me dictated. Call the secretaries at once!"

Buncha took one glance at the crumpled parchment and she whispered in Pilate's ear. "It's been shaved, and that's the roll that you gave the Arab when, you know. . . . The girls and. . . ."

"True, true. It was never written by me. Go, Jew. Go back at once and tell them that the writing is false and that the treasure is safe. And also say that the vestments may be called for now at any time."

"Roman, you give us happy news. And your anger bespeaks truth. I go at once."

Then Buncha again whispered in Pilate's ear, and he called after him; "But the letter of gratitude that I sent to you I wrote myself. That I will never deny." He laughed.

Ben Rashid hurried to the Temple with his news.

The whole structure that Barzor built was crumbling and in another moment came crashing down as though an invisible Samson were pulling out the columns from within.

Barzor, a lonely rider against the setting sun,

298

went quietly on and on. Now he regretted that he had parted from Rongus and now he thought of Ezra his friend but he did not know that the learned rabbi was already dead. And other things also he did not know. But he rode on slowly and quietly and fairly well satisfied with his work. His horse paced wearily and the rider dreamed of distant places and of things long ago.

Suddenly before him he saw a long black line. He started. It looked as though a whole stratum of black jagged rocks had in a moment sprung from the ground. There were horses and riders and the lances that they carried caught the blood-red glint of the dying sun.

For an instant he stopped and looked more sharply. There were hundreds and hundreds of riders dressed in black iron mail with round sharply pointed helmets.

They rode like a black wave on a yellow sea. And all before them, the Arab tribes, and even the wild jackals of the desert fled like the wind when they saw them coming.

"It's the Syrians!" he cried. And turning about he kicked into his horse and fled.

Once the horse stumbled. He was winded. He stumbled a second time. Once more his hoof caught in a briar but with unsteady legs he went on and on until he stumbled for the last time and came down with a final crash to the ground.

The Syrians! That savage black wave rolled on and on with wild calls and desert yells.

Barzor beside his fallen horse spoke softly to himself; "It is as my little wife said on that terrible night in Bethlehem, 'This is our end.' These words were hers and now they are mine too. In this we are together again. Let the ugly brutes come on."

XXV

THE Syrian army rested for three hours and then they went forward until midnight. Now they rested again and again they went on. With the first glimpse of dawn they saw the distant walls of Jerusalem.

But Buncha also kept a sharp outlook and with the coming dawn she saw the long lines of black lances. She awoke Pilate with the good news; "The Syrian army is here. They have come!"

Then she ran out to look again and came back with the news; "They come on like a black tide and with them is a prisoner! Soon they will be at the northern gate."

. . . .

Rongus had spent the night wandering about aimlessly, sometimes riding the weary horse and sometimes leading him by the bridle. How it was, he could not explain but with the coming of dawn he found himself within view of the city of Jerusalem. He knew he was not to come near this place. He remembered the warning but something drew him on.

When the sun sent forth its first rays Rongus saw the walls and towers from the south, for he was not far from the doors called the Fountain Gate. Now he thought of a plan. He tied the horse in a small grove of palm trees and went forward cautiously. He could see from the distance that the doors were still closed and nobody could be seen about.

He sat down on a stone and rested. His simple mind was confused. Presently he drew his dagger and cut his cloak in many places. After this was done he rolled in the dust and mud of the road until his hands and face and garments resembled those of a slovenly beggar. Thus disguised, nobody would recognize him and he could go to the place. . . . That very special place and find . . .

Then Rongus decided that it was too early and went back to the grove where he had tied the horse. But soon he heard the horns and he knew the doors would be open. Now he went forward again and risked all.

The city was now bursting with life. The visitors, the pilgrims, the devouts, the tradesmen and beggars all were now to be found here. All were preparing for the Passover. The bakers worked like mad and the vendors of meats and greens did a thriving business. Beggars were everywhere crying out with their plaintive voices.

Then there was a great commotion in the main street. Some cried one thing and others called out against them. Roman soldiers tramped with heavy step and shouted orders; "In the name of Cæsar, clear the way! On!"

They had with them some person—a prisoner. Rongus did not see him but he heard the shouting and cursing and he saw an ugly mob going forward, laughing and jeering. They went in the direction of the Temple and he followed. But he kept a safe distance away from the Roman soldiers who were trying to keep the noisy rabble in order.

When he came to the steps of the Temple he looked about but he could not find Mariamne and her blind brother. He did however see, in the outer court, his despised uncle among the money-changers, and they were quarrelling among themselves about the loss of some money and some shouted so loud that he could hear them from where he stood. "We will go now and bear witness. . . ." one called. And another cried; "For shame. There is no one to protect us from these table-wreckers!"

He went quietly away because he feared that his uncle might recognize him in spite of his besmeared appearance and fall upon him in revenge.

After walking warily about the booths and gay bazaars set up in the vicinity, he came back to the Temple steps. A small crowd was now gathered and Mariamne and David were in the center.

Rongus came closer. His heart leaped with joy.

David was seated on the Temple steps crying bitterly from the eyes that now could see the world. "It is not at all what I imagined it would be! It is poor and the colors are dull and nothing, nothing is as I thought."

304

"But David, my own beloved brother. We have found the prophet and he has just passed us with the angry crowd and the soldiers. He touched your head and. . . . Don't cry my beloved David. I will be with you and never leave you. I always knew it would happen and all our weary steps have not been in vain."

But the boy cried bitter tears; "The world is flooded with light but it is not what I thought it should look like."

"He can see!" called one. "It is truly a miracle."

But there were some who did not believe and they held their fingers up before his eyes; "Say how many you see." And each time the boy looking out through his tears gave the proper number.

"It is true. He can see!" And some shrugged their shoulders and went about their business.

Now Rongus edged his way through the small gathering until he stood directly behind Mariamne.

"I am also here," he said softly.

She turned quietly and threw her arms about him.

"No greater joy has ever come to me. And both have come within a single hour. Oh, Rongus! Whole nights I was awake hoping and wishing. And now you are safe. Oh, Rongus!"

But before he could reply two soldiers laid hands upon him.

"In the name of Cæsar," they ordered.

But he broke himself loose and with his great strength he had almost thrown them off and fled. More came upon him and overpowered him. They dragged him away.

Now a beggar, some wild fellow who had come down from the hills to gather a few coins from the holiday crowd, sat by the side of the steps and cried out in a voice loud and clear; "All for a penny and a penny for all. And the world will go as the penny goes."

Mariamne and David ran after.

"Oh, Rongus, Rongus," cried Mariamne. "What have you done?"

"I don't know! I don't know!"

But the soldiers thrust the brother and sister back.

And the beggar called aloud; "And silver and gold will be the gods. Love and pity are no more. All for a penny and a penny for all."

306

XXVI

THE high priests held their own court at the house of Caiaphas but the power to condemn prisoners to death had been taken away from them.

Pilate held his court in the open between the stone steps of the Towers and the bridge that arched over into the barracks. Here under a gay awning he sat and judged all brought before him. And it was here that Rongus was taken immediately on his arrest.

There was still a noisy crowd about and they argued among themselves. Some cried; "It is just, it is right," and others said, "It is only envy of the Temple priests," and to this some answered; "Blas-

phemy!" The condemned prisoner was led away.
A crowd was about him.

Now Rongus stood before Pilate.

"This is the other one!" cried the soldiers. "Now
we have both."

"In this case I will not be compelled to do the
will of anyone but myself. I have seen him myself
before and I know. I will need no water to wash
my hands in the presence of the people. No unjust
blood is spilt here. Take him away with the others.
Crucify him!"

.   .   .   .

Calvary.

The little hill outside about a hundred paces
beyond the North gate.

Two crosses already stood black against the sky.
The third was on the ground.

Barzor hung on the outer cross and Rongus saw
him and called out to him; "Oh master! Why did
we ever part? Why did you free me for this?"

The Arab replied in a clear strong voice; "Every
man must taste death at least once. I taste it twice.
Once with Herod and now with you."

But when the soldiers threw Rongus down upon the cross they ripped his outer garments away and there behold! was the golden breast-plate. This they quickly unstrapped and they struggled between themselves for its possession.

"All or nothing!" cried one soldier. "I'll cast lots with you."

"No lots. Cut it up and divide."

"Break it now. I want my share."

"All or nothing. High man wins!"

But then the captains came forward and ordered the soldiers to go on with their task.

When Rongus was securely tied with ropes, the cross was lifted and set into a hole in the ground that was there for this purpose.

Now three crosses stood against the gray sky. These were no broken teeth of a monster's comb for a sky of tangled locks. These were no rocky tombs like those of Egypt for a few weazened dead.

A strange light came upon it all. The sky sank away hollow like a great cave of black ashen chalk streaked with strange lines of light traced by a fingerless hand. The sun was blotted out.

309

And Mariamne came in great anguish upon the scene and wept.

But the soldiers quarrelled among themselves for the possession of the golden breast-plate. And they broke it into pieces with a mallet that was on the ground and then they played dice for the squares of gold. Some had skins of wine that had just come from Rome with the saved treasure and they drank lustily. Others drank their light grape vinegar and spit mouthfuls before them.

A strange light poured over the torture-capped mound. Faces glowed with a light that penetrated all. Here were the Romans one by one. Faces:— Ugly toil, corruption, iron in flesh and water in spirit, lips and eyes in an oblique shift. And the two with spears who stood guard, both were feeble brutes of huge bulk. And here the captains:—One a half-girl fellow and the other a Roman with a white boiling eye and a face of warty spite.

"Pay me the money!" cried one.

"I don't owe it."

"Yes, you do," came the coarse reply. "You do, I gave it to you when we met in the stews, for you wanted the she-jinks with the scissor legs."

"It's a lie!"

"Say it again and I'll hit you a blood-blow."

They were separated by their comrades.

Now all was dark, dark, and only the shadows could be seen and that blaze of pain.

Were these wooden beams for a temple?

．　　．　　．　　．　　．　　．　　．

The shadows were thick and trance-like. And great red bulks filled the sky—a bridge of molten iron for phantom figures to cross. And there against the sky—was that a black dog with yellow eyes, followed by a fawn-colored horse without a rider? And is that a peddler of mirrors for cool vanity? Drive him away!

And there are noises, strange and distant. Will a sounding brass call out a sweet word? Will a dream rule the world? Can tears melt sorrow?

"Oh!" called Rongus. "What have I done to deserve this?"

"Forgive me Rongus," said Barzor. But now his limbs were white and his voice was feeble.

A streak of light came filtering through the sky.

But the soldiers still quarrelled among themselves,

their drunken voices loud and strong, and their language vile.

But Rongus had been a slave and he was strong in muscle and bone, stronger than any. It was long until he too fell limp and his form could no longer bear the burden of the cross.

Now the mad Sulla—where he had been all this while nobody knows—came running upon the scene.

"Ah!" he cried. "How now brothers! Oh! How long I have waited for this!"

With these words he put up the short ladder and snatched the wooden mallet. Then he mounted, and pounded with all his might until he broke all the bones in Barzor's body. Then he carried the ladder across the mound to the place where Rongus hung and he broke his bones too.

This was the end.

.   .   .   .

In the Towers, Mariamne kneeled before Pilate and wept. Buncha led her away and tried to console her. She put her arm about her and said; "No one can teach an orphan how to weep."

312

When the Babylonian dwarf returned to the long
hall, Pilate said to her; "Oh, Buncha! How weary
I am! The air is thick. It is stifling. Jerusalem is
fusty. Let us be off to the palace in Cæsarea. There
the air has the brace of the sea and I will look out
upon it and know that the same water washes the
shores of Rome. Tell the women to get ready, for
tomorrow we can start."

Then he called the Latin secretaries and ordered
them to write a scroll. He dictated; "To Imperator Tiberius Cæsar in Rome. All is peaceful in
Judea and there is little to do."

He took the ring from his finger and pressed
his seal to the parchment.

PS3521.O53 T9   c.1
Komroff, Manuel, 189   100107 000
Two thieves / Manuel Komroff.

3 9310 00063148 9
GOSHEN COLLEGE-GOOD LIBRARY